A Novel

TRITON'S
ZODIAC

D1416892

ISBN 978-1-58776-191-1

1. (Historical Fiction)

Library of Congress catalog card number: 2013955830

Manufactured in the United States of America

NetPublications, Inc

HUDSON HOUSE PUBLISHING

675 Dutchess Turnpike,
Poughkeepsie, NY 12603
(800) 724-1100
www.hudsonhousepub.com

A Novel

TRITON'S ZODIAC

Candano

To Jane,
the flowers you care
for are almost as
lovely as you are
and always
have been.
Love,
Christine

C. A. Dano

author of *The Hourglass*

Acknowledgments

Special thanks to: my esteemed editor, Ann LaFarge; Irish Szary, cherished friend and computer guru; my son, Dennis Rovnak, for creating the author photo; and to my husband, Michael, with whom all good things are possible.

For WJS,
The Golden Child

Prologue
The Hamptons, Long Island
September 21, 1938

*I*t *would go down in history as one of the worst disasters ever to hit the eastern seaboard. It was also to become a legendary basis for the nightmares New Englanders would have for generations to come. A storm of intense magnitude, encapsulating sand and sea life, its path of destruction when it finally hit down would geographically redefine the land. But first, there was the party—Westhampton's social event of the year...*

The ingenuity of President Franklin D. Roosevelt had birthed The March of Dimes—the newest, most celebrated non-profit organization to date. Every investor, philanthropist and politician seeking recognition or looking to bury a portion of their profit margin in a tax-free organization was involved in its mission. Many of these entrepreneurial tycoons now gathered on the majestic beachfront property belonging to one of their own. It was the intent of the foundation that attendees would willingly donate hefty sums of cash or pen a generous amount from their company checkbooks.

So lavish was the party that no one seemed to mind when, sometime in the mid-afternoon, the very air they were breathing stopped moving. To say it was the calm before the storm would be an understatement. No one recognized it as the pending demolition it was to become; but even if they had, it would already have been too late.

It began with a light shower. Within minutes, needle-sharp raindrops were pelting down from the sky as fast as machine gun fire. The men hurriedly escorted the ladies to protective cover under the canopy of the big white tent.

One woman, wearing an enormous black straw hat adorned with a yellow rose, refused to let a little rain ruin her day. She had survived the very disease funds were being raised for; surely she could withstand a little soaking. Raising her glass in a mock toast with one hand and securing her chapeau with the other, she declared the shower a prophetic omen of good luck.

The undulating clouds, already dark and foreboding, answered her salute by shifting and swirling. They parted to reveal a murky, mustard-colored sky whose dooming hue steamrolled across the bay, spewing forth a furious wind that sounded as if it had been sent up from the bowels of hell.

The rainfall increased until it became a woeful torrential downpour, banefully accompanied by eighty-mile-an-hour winds that sent tables and chairs flying. A shrieking stampede ensued as terrified guests frantically pushed and shoved their way toward the dining tent now teetering perilously in the deadly caterwaul that had barreled across a fulminating sea.

Band equipment was hurled from the lawn and sent up into the darkening sky. Two musicians were lifted, as if by some an invisible force, and sucked away into the shrieking vortex. The tent poles, straining under the gravitational pull, finally snapped, their thick long ropes whipping as deadly as electrical wires. In minutes, the tent was hoisted in its entirety and ballooned into the atmosphere like an enormous white jellyfish.

Some guests were trampled in an effort to reach the main house, their feeble cries for help drowned out by the insane howling of a merciless wind. Several more were mowed down by flying debris, three of them dying instantly when the catastrophic winds ripped a twenty-foot pine from the ground, its root system still fully intact, and sent it spiraling sideways across the ravaged yard.

Shingles and shutters were violently torn from the house to fly in the air as crippling and deadly as shrapnel. The automobiles parked along the driveway rocked and teetered; two of them tumbled, like clothes in a dryer, down the street and out of sight. Guests who managed to reach the house shoved their way up the wide stone steps of the porch to burst through the great entryway in desperate search for a safe place to hide.

Glass shattered as windows were sucked from their panes by the sudden explosion of wind that levitated furniture and sent it crashing into walls. At the peak of the storm, the all-consuming wind peeled back a small portion of roof from the grand homestead, loosening the tented housetop from its supporting beams.

The captive hostages found themselves exposed to a deadly horror above them. They screamed, as the cyclonic hurricane glowered down on them, calling to the sea to raise a moving mountain of water which in minutes had covered the beach and crossed the lawn.

The wall of water loomed where only moments before a ceiling had existed. It was a mammoth wave, beating with a life of its own and towering fifty feet above in a deadly cobra stance. The last tormented cries of those huddled below it were lost beneath the deafening roar as the horrific descent of the water wall, like one great demonic claw, obliterated the crippled estate, inhaling it entirely into its lethal hydraulic abyss.

Cape Cod, Massachusetts

Summer, 1937

A year before the storm...

Catherine

It's the same lemon meringue pie recipe I've used for years, but this time I've burned the crust on one, and the filling in the other is lumpy. It would not fare well for the minister's wife to present ruined pies to our church's annual bake sale; I'm going to have to start over again from scratch. William is undoubtedly going to hold me accountable for being wasteful (the cost of the ingredients and use of extra electric) and he will be justified in doing so.

No wonder I've ruined the pies, for I have thought of little else but Jack's letter, which arrived for me not two weeks ago. It came addressed to *Mrs. Catherine McFarley,* hastily sprawled across the envelope in the lackadaisical scribble I can still remember Jack's penmanship to be, and with only the initials *J.W.* in the upper corner to identify the sender. No return address. Typical Jack—not wanting anyone to know where he is or where he's been for the past sixteen years.

If I have read his letter once, I have read it a thousand times. Every word is emblazoned in my brain, and I can think of little else other than how to tell William about it.

My love and affection for two men seems acceptable to me; but only one, William, is my lawful husband, and he is not a tolerant man when it comes to the subject of Jack Wakefield or the feelings I have for him.

This I understand, for William married me without reservation when I was pregnant with Jack's child. He loved me enough to give me his name, to be a father to my unborn baby, and to offer us a safe haven in an upstanding parish home. But the sanctuary William offered came with a price: my youth, and the capricious reverie that should have been part of it.

Years ago, my neighbor and dearest friend, Frances Gellermont, asked what it was like to be married to a preacher. I had been married just a short time when she posed the question and, therefore, could not answer her truthfully.

If she were to ask me today, I would have her feel the heart of a captured woodland sparrow, pulsing warm and elusively in her palms, only to have the bird suddenly fly off, so that she would be left to wonder if she had even held it at all. Or I would ask if she has ever experienced the catapult of being driven to the brink of despair, only to discover she has been left alone there, in utter isolation, to self-soothe her fears and sorrows alone. I would have her sip seawater from a shell; and when the salty taste of it made her grimace, I would offer her cool, sweet cream to cleanse her palate.

Only after experiencing such things could Frances even begin to fathom the highs and lows, the trials and tribulations of my relationship with William McFarley.

And then, there is Jack Wakefield. Even I cannot begin to grasp or comprehend what was between us, much less express what I still feel after so many years gone by.

I never doubted that Jack thought himself a respectable man, or that he wanted to do right by me. But in the end, gentleman or cad, he left me pregnant and without recourse. Jack loved me, I know he did, but he loved something else more. He loved it more than his unborn child; he loved it even more than himself. When my belly rounded so that I could no longer keep our baby a secret, I confronted Jack. I insisted that he make a choice. In the end, Jack sailed away. He was utterly in love with, and caught up in, the bewitching, infinitesimal depths of my arch rival: the sea.

Ask how I can still be in love with the man who left me in my greatest hour of need rather than devote myself entirely to the man who came to my rescue—the one who provided me with a respectable sanctuary to disguise what most would have called shameful, but which I will forever secretly affirm as my most consequential triumph? I cannot say. What I do know for sure is that there are two women in my head. One wears red and longs for the rapscallion sailor who evokes immeasurable passion in her; the other is garbed in white and delights in the protection of a minister's safekeeping.

At parity, there are also two men in my heart. One is the father of my son; the other, my son's father.

I caress the smooth page of Jack's letter resting inside my apron pocket. I trace my finger over the ridged edge of postage while envisioning him far out at sea and imagine myself an equal distance away. My husband's understanding is a short rope, and I am at a disadvantage in how to broach the subject of Jack's letter.

How do I tell William that, after nearly seventeen years, Jack Wakefield, who knew all along that he had fathered a child, has now decided to sail home to meet that son for the first time?

Frances

The debilitating affliction of childhood polio renders me no more helpless than having married an established name affords me comfort. The polished pew I am sitting in, just as most of this well-provisioned church, exists thanks to the over-abundant generosity of my late husband, Bentley Rellerford Gellermont IV, a penniless Bostonian blueblood until he married me in 1902.

When Reverend William McFarley announces, "Please stand for the word of Our Lord," I do not. I cannot, not without making much to-do with my crutches. Since both my position and condition are recognized as permanent fixtures in this town, I remain seated, like a queen. A queen need not follow protocol.

I am, however, no different from anyone else when it comes to worshiping Our Lord. Earnestly I try to concentrate on the scripture reading and the laborious sermon following, both fervently delivered by our dear pastor in full crescendo.

"It is not of our Savior's choosing when lives are lost to tragedy," Reverend McFarley clearly states, "and it is the strong of heart that do not blame God Almighty for it, but rather, ask His grace upon those souls lost to catastrophe. Afterward, we must rejoice; for those faithful souls have been delivered on angels' wings, to live for eternity in the Glory of God, The Father."

The Reverend's reference to the thirty five passengers of the Hindenburg, all of whom lost their lives when the German airship ignited and crashed over New Jersey just two months ago, is his attempt at diplomacy for an historical event that everyone views as Germany's greatest debacle to date. Lord forgive me for wishing this depressing homily to end, but I long to go home, where I can look forward to sipping a cool glass of lemonade under the shaded veranda of my porch that overlooks the sea.

For all his awe-inspiring presence and humility, Reverend McFarley is unvarying when he preaches. For years, the man has been respected by his peers and regarded with favor by his parishioners. We are, each one of us, impressed by his devotion to God's work and to the general well being of our community during these uncertain economic times. And as a frequent guest in the McFarley household, I can attest to the Reverend's seemingly endless energy and untiring dedication to serving God, government, and flock. For this reason alone I should be diligent and alert in my attention to the sermon, but I find my thoughts wandering again, this time to a somewhat questionable but far more intriguing distraction seated beside me; namely, Catherine McFarley and her children. That they are the pastor's family is of lesser importance than the fact that Catherine is the dearest woman and my most trusted confidante.

Catherine's manner is gentle and unassuming, yet I have known her to be forthright and, dare I say, downright stubborn when she believes she is in the right. There is a certain riddle about Catherine that I gravitate toward, as well as a captivating persona that helps me forget the physical bondage of my handicap. Plainly put, Catherine has a way about her that makes me feel whole and uninhibited.

She is alluring in her complexity. I find her company most enjoyable and her children well behaved. It is never a chore to share the front pew with them. In fact, for years now, I have made sure to position my crutches lengthwise on the seat of the pew so that we four may have it completely to ourselves.

Being the wife of a minister, Catherine takes churchgoing seriously. However, I notice that today she has been preoccupied since the service began. I see her turning her head every so often to look past her son and stare out the stained glass window nearest her.

Every window in the church has been opened wide to let in what little breeze there is on this midsummer morning of unfaltering heat and humidity. My friend is as unmoving as one of the marble statues in front of us. Between her ethereal features and fixed gaze, Catherine resembles Rita Hayworth in one of her more lamentable roles. Only the slightest movement of the limp netting that edges her hat, along with a springy auburn curl that has managed to escape from under it, brings reality to her seemingly sculpted pose.

Clearly, there is little view for her to engage in, save the abundant lower branches of the aged oak tree (an enormity that has outlived the structure it shades by a hundred years) and a few hydrangea bushes badly in need of pruning. Their heavy vibrant blue crowns rest listlessly upon the windowsill as if observing my friend, whose thoughts seem to extend far beyond her view.

I lean slightly forward just in time to catch a faint smile pass Catherine's lips. The smile is an unquestionable contradiction to her hands, which are folded primly and resolutely upon her lap. Whatever dream she is conjuring, she is undoubtedly in it. *Will it be worth the reprimand she is bound to receive later from her husband?* I wonder, for the Reverend has noticed her vague stare. I imagine he guesses that his wife's mind is on a fanciful run.

Sitting on either side of Catherine are her two children: Jonah is sixteen; Elizabeth, otherwise referred to as *Lizzie,* has recently turned eleven. It appears that the heat of summer has gotten the best of one of them.

Elizabeth dozes, limp as a ragdoll, propped against her mother's shoulder. Tiny beads of perspiration dampen her curls, turning them from light to dark brown. The temperature inside the church has deepened the flush on her usually petal-pink cheeks, raising it to a feverish crimson.

Her brother, Jonah, sits hovering over his prayer book. He wears an expression intense with intrigue that only helps to enhance a sinfully handsome face, yet it rather puts me in mind of a cat ready to devour a mouse.

Apart from the fact that he is as fine-looking as the knave in a deck of cards, I find young master McFarley's concentration to prayer less than genuine. I am no expert on men, young or old, but I should think a boy of Jonah's age would be directing his attention to young Alice Brighton, sitting across the aisle from us. Clearly her mother must be blind to have let her daughter out of the house wearing a blouse cut so blatantly low that her bosoms resemble two toasted honey buns. I look from Alice to Jonah, but the boy appears oblivious.

Jonah is a vision of monastic spirituality. He keeps his eyes, as equine as a colt's, transfixed on the written word as if he cannot absorb enough of it. His future has been pre-ordained to follow in his father's footsteps, but personally, I do not believe the boy's heart is really in it; and if that be the case, his reverent demeanor could merely be a ruse to placate his father.

13

When it is time for the collection, Jonah rises from his seat to help assist with the passing of the baskets. Working his way from the back of the tiny church and down the aisle, he finally reaches the first pew and holds the basket parallel to my chest. As I remove the folded bills from my purse and deposit them in the basket, I believe I see the slightest trembling of Jonah's hand, but perhaps not.

The passing of the communal bread is a swift and painless ordeal. The day is too stifling for even the most devout, and our prayers are finally answered when Reverend McFarley stands before us to deliver his parting blessing:

"Pray, brothers and sisters, that today we have received God's word; that we keep our hearts open to His calling; and that we ask His blessing and His mercy to fall upon us. Amen."

The congregation replies with a wilted *Amen* as the organist, Bernice Clapton, brings the ceremony to a close with a thunderous rendition of *Be Ye Transformed*.

Catherine, who transports me to church most Sundays, gracefully steps out from the pew and into the aisle.

"Frances, will you be riding home with us?"

"I would, but I have offered some day lilies to Edwina Dougherty. They are running rampant in the garden this year, and Edwina could use a bouquet for her dinner company this afternoon."

"All right then, we will catch up tomorrow," Catherine promises. "This afternoon I'm helping William with the monthly ledgers, but I'll be sure to send Elizabeth over with a dessert for after your dinner—-a nice warm biscuit with fresh blueberries and clotted cream."

"I'll be taking my garments to the seamstress to have the waists widened if you don't curb that baking," I reply, always touched by her kindness. "But you know I appreciate it and will love every bite."

Catherine motions Elizabeth to move on. She bids me good day, and I watch admiringly as she walks behind the shadow of her elusive son, who had already completed his own hasty exit up the narrow aisle.

It takes several minutes to affix the metal bands of my crutches around both forearms. Only then do I happen to notice the prayer book lying where Jonah accidentally left it.

It is a well-worn copy with a leather patina as smooth as a newborn's skin. I am surprised to see upon closer inspection that the original contents have been carefully cut out of the book's binding and another volume inserted in its place. I gently pull on the thin faded ribbon that marks his page and the aged prayer book falls open in my palm.

There are no verses of scripture, no words of adoration for the angels and saints. Instead, I am looking at a crisp copy of C. S. Forester's new sea-faring tale, *The Happy Return*, complete with Jonah's marginal notes and miniature ink sketches of *Horatio Hornblower* in his official Royal Naval uniform. I admit I am unsure just what to make of it.

Jonah

I am a puzzle no one seems to be able to piece together, but I also believe I am worth the try.

Once, when I was old enough to know better, I cut down a sapling spruce from a neighbor's yard to serve as our family Christmas tree. When he heard how I had gone about getting it, my father first gave me the strap before ordering me to hack all but two of the branches from the tree, while he stood watching, until the sorry shaft resembled a crucifix. My father then made me drag the desecrated tree all the way to our church and tie it to the railing, along with a sign in my own handwriting. *Thou shall not covet thy neighbor's goods,* it read. Then he made me sign my name to it.

Father has never tolerated any sin against man or nature, yet I am forever testing him. Sometimes I stand outside myself and wonder how my father, such an honorable man, came to have me (such a bugger) for a son.

Mother, too, deserved a son less troublesome than I have been for her. It is in a mother's nature to forgive. Mine continually throws me that nurturing lifeline, and inevitably I grab on to it—if only to (hypothetically) use it to hang myself.

My mother believes I am destined to do great things. I wish I could say I agree with her. Where she finds her faith in me is anyone's guess. The only thing I am totally sure of is that I will forever test the patience of both my mother and father.

Apart from me and my role as the *bad* child, there is something going on between my parents. I know because they haven't been acting right for weeks now, and I've been able to get away with a lot of stuff they would have caught if their minds were not occupied with something else. I have no clue as to what it could be.

Earlier tonight, when Mother was putting Lizzie to bed, Father went in my sister's room to kiss her goodnight. I heard him and Mother having words. I put my ear to the wall but couldn't make out what they were saying. Still, there was no mistaking the heated tone of their exchanges. I can only hope that whatever it was that they were arguing about has nothing to do with me.

It could have something to do with my mother's best friend, Mrs. Gellermont, showing up a week ago unannounced. She had arrived looking stern, her eyebrows joined together in the middle, and her mouth pulled as thin and tight as a paper cut. Whatever the reason, it was serious enough to bring the 'ol girl out on her crutches.

She had crossed our lawn with the purpose of a linebacker, her uneven walk bringing to mind the sea crabs my buddies and me try to catch down on the beach when tide's out. One look at her expression and I thought for sure she had discovered the missing money. A flash picture of my father being told of my thievery nearly caused my knees to buckle, but I guess it was my lucky day. For as it turned out, Mrs. Gellermont had only come to return my prayer book, though she was clearly upset with my altering of it. She opened it up and held it out to for my mother to see as if I had drawn dirty pictures on the pages. It was just some innocent sketches of a fighter ship and some uniforms.

Mother tried making excuses for me.

"Oh, Frances, you know how boys are. Why Horatio Hornblower is all the rage nowadays."

But the old girl wasn't to be put off. Mrs. Gellermont believed I needed punishing and told my mother as much.

"Catherine, you cannot make light of this! The boy has been earmarked for the ministry," she barked. "What would William say if he knew his son was reading trivial text in place of gospel?"

Earmarked? Who uses words like that? I saw my mother's eyes dance lightly, as they often do, with an irresistible softness. She added a crooked smile and offered a disciplinary olive branch.

"I will personally see to it that Jonah makes his prayer book right by next Sunday, Frances."

"See that he does," our neighbor said briskly, swiveling on one crutch to cast a knowing glance at me. She had my number.

I remember sheepishly raking a hand through my hair (a move that always works well on girls) and hanging my head, trying my best to appear contrite.

Mrs. Gellermont wrinkled her brow, pursing her narrow lips until they all but disappeared.

"I will see you tomorrow then."

And with that, she turned to leave. Only then did I exhale the breath I had been holding.

"Jonah, please see Mrs. Gellermont home."

I had rolled my eyes at Mother, and she widened her own in a silent expression of disapproval that told me I was not yet off the hook.

Mother never reported the incident to my father, but Mrs. Gellermont indeed checked my prayer book the following Sunday just to be sure it was a clean copy. Annoyed at her for not trusting me, I pocketed two bills from her contribution to the church basket instead of the usual one that I had been helping myself to each week.

It wasn't long after the prayer book incident that two of my buddies, Rick Slater and Kevin Granner, and I got caught smoking in school. I wouldn't have thought so, but Father went fairly easy on me when he found out. He said it was only natural a lad should want to try smoking and then proceeded to lecture me about the *sin of indulgence*—in this particular case, smoking and drinking. Wouldn't he have a fit if he knew I've been doing both since I was ten?

Tonight, though, Father and I are having a decent go of it. He promised if I completed my homework and agreed to an hour of bible study we could listen to the radio premier of *The Shadow.* I've diligently pressed my head to the academic and religious grindstones; and when he finally notices the anxious pumping of my knee, he checks his watch and motions that we can end our session.

Mother is already in the living room, where she has set up the ironing board and has the new Steam-O-Matic electric iron we gave her for her birthday plugged in and heated. A basket of fresh-smelling laundry is at her feet, and she is absentmindedly folding and separating the clothes inside it.

For years, that mysterious voice we are all anxiously waiting to hear was the narrator on the original program, *Detective Story*. I never got to hear it unless I happened to be with a friend whose parents owned a radio. Our family would still be without one if my father's congregation hadn't pooled their money to give him one last year. It's a Sears Silvertone, with a gold tuning eye dial to mark the company's 50 years in business. The radio is the best Christmas gift Father ever got from his parishioners. It's definitely better than one of Mrs. Wilbur's disgusting fruitcakes (which we always give away) or some ugly necktie, which my father will always graciously accept when he's given one but then never wear.

The radio announcer is calling tonight's episode, *The Death House Rescue*. In it The Shadow possesses the power to cloud men's minds so they can't see him. I'm sitting on the floor, fidgeting with readiness. I've got a handful of freshly-baked oatmeal cookies and a glass of milk to wash them down with. If only my sister would stay in bed! Mother left Lizzie's bedroom door part way open, just like she makes sure to do every night, and from here I can see my sister's head sticking out to sneak a peek. She is not one to miss out on a family gathering and will catch the show even if it means eavesdropping. I hide the cookies from view.

My mother places her iron on the hot plate. She looks at me and says:—

"Jonah, if you are going to sit on the floor, please move that glass before it gets knocked over. And use your napkin when you dunk cookies."

Geez! Why don't you just shout it? All Lizzie has to hear is that she's missing out on having dessert. I swear that kid can hear a pin drop.

I am thinking that after the program, I might sneak out behind the shed for a smoke. Maybe then I'll be able to figure out what The Shadow would have done had his father tried pushing him toward the ministry instead of allowing him to become the famous vigilante he is today. Father believes our country is headed for war. If his prediction is true, I could do more good by joining the Navy than becoming a minister. I'd have to enlist secretly, though. Mother would never let me enter the service without putting up a fight.

We hear that chilling voice suddenly come over the radio. It speaks the words we've been waiting to hear: *"Who knows what evil lurks in the hearts of men? The Shadow knows!"* Those words, spoken with a haunting laugh and spooky music, never fail to send a shiver up my spine.

I quickly glance at my parents and then over at my sister, still stationed at her bedroom door, hungrily eyeing the last cookie on my plate. As unfinished a puzzle as I may be, there's no family I'd rather be a part of; no family I'd rather be sitting with at this moment.

I down the last of my milk and lean in closer to the base of my father's chair.

Catherine

Jack Wakefield. He was roguishly handsome, devilishly irresistible, and impossible to deny. We met the summer I turned thirteen. Jack was fifteen.

I am an only child. I had lost my mother to consumption just three years before. Back then, my father, a music teacher in Manhattan, took the advice of an associate teacher and began vacationing with me each summer on Cape Cod, where his teacher friend convinced him that sea air would rejuvenate a grieving heart.

Jack and his parents were Cape residents as was Jack's best friend, William McFarley, and his family. Every summer for the next three years, Jack and William wholeheartedly accepted the addition of an uptown girl, welcoming me into their tightly-knit duo of camaraderie. They were gentlemen when I was in their presence and kept their patience with me, an outsider, though I cannot help but think that in due time both lived to regret having done so.

My father rented the same cottage for us every summer. It was a small two-bedroom dwelling, with shingles bleached by the salt air and a screen door that slammed shut every time it was opened. What yard there was consisted of nothing more than sandy soil, with sparse patches of dried grass for lawn; but for my father and me, who walked the hard pavement of city streets ten months a year, those arid summer tufts were as luxurious as turf on a ritzy suburban golf course.

An antiquated split-rail fence bordered our marginal lot. Sitting on that fence with my toes touching the brambling lingonberry plants that clung in deeply-hued clusters against it and gazing upon the distant nautical horizon was always the first thing I did after Father and I arrived and had finished unloading the car.

Rain or shine, I could always depend on the pungent aroma of the nearby marshland—dank, with tiny crustaceans burrowed deep in its mud, along with rotting shells and various forms of algae. All of it was responsible for maintaining the natural balance in a hidden underworld that pulsated with life and procreated century after century for the observation and enjoyment of those people who lived there.

We found Cape Cod to have a heartbeat all of its own. To *live it* was to drink it in and allow it to course through our veins like life's blood.

The Wakefields lived next door to us and the McFarleys just a street behind. It wasn't long before their parents welcomed my father into their homes, frequently inviting him to join in a game of cards or a lobster bake on the beach. Parental discussions centered around their personal opinion of President Woodrow Wilson, who had been narrowly re-elected just two years before, in 1916. While our fathers debated the pros and cons of Wilson's Federal Reserve Act and his Federal Trade Commission Act, the wives praised him for being the great advocate he was for women's suffrage.

Two Saturday evenings a month during the summer, Jack's father would talk William's into squandering a ration of their earnings and treating their wives to an evening at the cinema. Father was uncomfortable with their insistence he join them; my mother's passing had left a void no activity could fill. A film, or listening to local ragtime music was a tempting rouse, and our motorcar was the most spacious. And so, after some persuasion, father would agree to drive his rowdy passengers, who in turn would stick their heads out of the car windows, whistling and cheering, each one heady with the freedom from the bondage of parenthood.

On those nights when he went out, Father would hire our neighbor, the decrepit Mrs. Gibson, to be home for me. Ruddy Mrs. Gibson smelled of camphor and, often times, of gin. But she ruled with a sturdy hand and charged less than most; therefore, she was my father's first choice as a competent protector.

My curfew was a firm nine o'clock, and when Father was gone I was instructed to stay within earshot of Mrs. Gibson's bawdy instruction. But Jack and William were shrewd. They knew all the tricks for keeping me out beyond the witching hour and played Mrs. Gibson like the crackerjacks they were.

One night, while Jack and I hid in the bushes outside, Will hammered his fist on our front door, anxiously reporting to an alarmed Mrs. Gibson that he thought he could smell smoke coming from her house. Had Jack told her the same lie, the old woman would have been on to him. William, however, had the angelic face every adult trusted. While the tipsy woman scurried next door to check on her home, Will signaled us. Together, Jack and I rushed upstairs to my bedroom, where we grabbed the clothes lying on the floor and stuffed them under the bed sheets to resemble my slumbering form. Their prankster game worked like a charm and probably sent Mrs. Gibson straight to the bottle, but we three had a ball. Sometime after midnight, the boys watched from the ground while I climbed the side trellis and snuck in through the window Jack had been sure to leave open as the final touch to our devious charade.

As trusted by his elders as William was, Jack had an opposite effect on adults. William often spoke of his and Jack's shenanigans, like how their teacher, Miss Forrester, had Jack's number from the very first. Try as he might, apparently Jack could not get too much past Miss Forrester. She was acutely aware of his academic potential and expected Jack to toe the mark along with the rest of the class. Miss Forrester often suspected him of having someone else do his homework and sometimes would call him on it. William said that when she did, Jack would simply flash her one of his irresistible expressions or bring her a paltry bouquet of wild flowers in place of an assignment, and inevitably be forgiven. William always said that Jack Wakefield knew how to play the girls. Little did I know.

Summers were exotic for the three of us. Youth and vitality were our passports to oblivion against changing times. We asked for nothing more than this paradise—a curving peninsula off Massachusetts—known simply as The Cape. Here we had everything we needed to feel alive, and we lived those summer days with a zest for discovery and a passion for the unknown.

While our parents lay awake at night, sleepless with the image of America's involvement should there be a second world war, their children's sleep was uninterrupted. We dreamed of foaming surf, pulsating with fascinating and unusual sea life; of standing ankle deep in blood-red cranberry bogs at harvest time; or of being the first to tempt a scurrying sandpiper on the beach to venture close enough to eat from our hand. In those days, the only difference between maturity and youth was, quite simply, reality versus fantasy. We let our parents do the worrying.

"Last one in is a rotten egg!" Jack would call to us as he dove, head first, into a frigid sea while William and I were still full yards behind him, running breathlessly to catch up.

We had dubbed ourselves *The Sea Urchins*, wiling away as many hours in the water as we could get away with. It amused the boys to see my skin turn from the pasty-white pallor of an urban girl to golden honey, which by their standards was still considered pale. By summer's end, William was as brown as a cup of weak tea; but Jack, whose swarthy skin had color even in dead of winter, could have passed for Al Jolson in his vocal rendition of *Mammy*.

The three of us swam nearly every day, even in the rain. Nothing short of a lightning bolt could keep us from the water, though none of us fared well if a mother was forced to trek down to the beach to wave us in with the onset of a storm rapidly rolling in across a threatening sky.

Jack taught me to paddle out beyond the breakers and trust the cresting waves to carry me back to shore. Buoying the swells to catch a ride was thrilling, until that inevitable moment when my timing would go awry and the mighty power of the waves would slam into me with the solid force of a brick wall. Every time it happened, I was terrified, tumbling head over heels beneath the unforgiving weight of seawater. Whenever William was with us, he came to my rescue. Jack never would.

"That's how she'll learn!" he'd scream, above the onslaught of the waves, treading effortlessly in place as William ignored him and repeatedly disappeared beneath the frothing waters in search of a flailing limb.

We'd surface, William sputtering his anger at Jack for putting me at risk, while I, coughing and gulping for air, would rebelliously break free from his safe hold, frantically paddling toward Jack for another try at proving myself. It was years later before I realized just how dangerous it was to play friends against each other that way.

Fishing was another forte of Jack's, and by my second summer on Cape I was a competent fisherman. I became knowledgeable about the various species of fish, some of which my Father gutted and boned for our dinners, but most of which were thrown back when Jack remarked they were as small as smelts.

On my sixteenth birthday, Jack gifted his best fishing pole to me, which to me was even more than the cherry red Zenith girl's bike I had been wishing for and my father bought for me.

William, ever practical, felt I was in need of developing my femininity, so he said. He gave me a jar of Pond's Cold Cream and a volume of Elizabeth Barrett Browning's *Sonnets From The Portuguese*. It bothered him to realize I did not want the things other girls wanted, such as dresses, and jewelry, and such. He seemed incapable of grasping the preference of this city girl for the simple things in life: the stinging sensation of salt air on my sunburned face and the jubilance that comes from having a flopping fish fighting wildly at the end of a fishing line. William thought I deserved much more than I ever actually wanted.

It was in a pair of Jack's ill-fitting breeches that I learned to dig for clams. It was strenuous work, dragging our rakes through unmovable beds of saturated sand left in the wake of low tide. It seemed that just when our backs were at the breaking point, our efforts would be rewarded.

"Got 'em!" one of us would shout, feeling our biceps working against the extra weight on the end of our rakes.

Dropping down on our haunches, we would drive our hands deep into the soggy sand of each other's catch, rewarded with several hard-shelled delicacies. It was a heady feeling to carry home a bucketful of clams at the end of a day; wash them, shuck them, and then savor their rounded meaty centers while clam juice dribbled down our chins and onto our shirts.

Life was more structured for William, who was made to study scripture before dinner four evenings a week. While his nose was resolutely pressed to his books, Jack and I would race up the nearby dunes that rippled like ribbon candy high along the shoreline.

With the cuffs of Jack's pants rolled up, and the hem of my cotton dress tucked between my legs and secured in my belt so that I might run unhampered, Jack and I would roam the wide expanse of beach, leaving creviced memorials of footprints behind us as we pulled and clawed our way to the top of the grassy knoll. Total empowerment awaited us there. From thirty feet above, we lorded over an east-to-west vista spread out below us, as breathtakingly serene as any still life painting.

Every summer, Jack and I came to stand at this same spot, bracing ourselves against high winds that threatened to lift us, like kites, into a sky bruised pink and purple from the kiss of a setting sun.

We were rulers of our own universe back then, with the island birds as our loyal subjects. Herring gulls, northern gannets, and red-breasted mergansers circled high above us in an unending quest for food. We stood for lengths of time, watching the glorified precision of these winged acrobatic performers make aerial nose dives, with amazing accuracy, into the dancing whitecaps below. In an aerial ballet of fluent motion, the birds would time each descent, diving beneath the crests and immediately emerging triumphant, with a doomed fish flapping between their sharpened beaks.

The stench of outgoing tide and the piquant smell of raw fresh fish are aromas as heady to a New Englander and just as fragrant as any bouquet. Jack loved to inhale it. He would fill his lungs, shaking his head as if nothing could compare.

"Does this air smell great, or what?" he would challenge, and I would shudder, much less enthralled, as he repeatedly drew the pungent odors through his nostrils and hold them deep in his lungs.

Though the air just smelled foul to me, Jack's passion for it was riveting to witness, with his smile so wide I could not help but fib, nodding my head in agreement. It was times like this, even enveloped as we were with the rank of low tide, that I would fall in love with him again, for the ten-thousandth time.

Just as the sea was Jack's love, she was also my competitor. Her charisma had gotten under his skin so undeniably that each summer I believed I could literally feel her invincible stronghold pulling Jack away—from me, from his family, from our beloved Cape Cod.

I always said it was not blood, but salt water, that ran through Jack Wakefield's veins. The power of the sea endlessly drew him toward her dark, fathomless mysteries. She drew him by means of her eternal tides, which ebbed and flowed from her undulating depths to reach beyond human flesh and confiscate one's very soul. From her vast global boundaries I knew, even when Jack did not, that the sea had begun to summon him with a chant only a sailor can hear. She eroded any chance we might have at love, just as she eroded the dunes with her endless, insatiable rhythms. Jack was weaker than the mightiness of the sea and her claim on him. He was hypnotized by her magnetism, and I was too in love with him not to try convincing him stay.

In time, Jack began spending the greater part of every day on his father's boat, departing at the break of dawn and not returning until late afternoon.

William, under duress, began devoting more of his spare time to his studies. Their absence was a tangible loss to me; and although William spent as much time with me as his schedule (and father) permitted, time with William was not what my heart craved, nor what I was longing for.

During that last summer together, Jack knew his best friend was in love with me. If he had an opinion about it one way or another, he never expressed it. Nor did Jack try to stand in William's way. He signed on as a crew member aboard an Alaskan-based trading vessel, severing all ties to Cape Cod with the simple stroke of his inked signature upon a binding contract. We saw each other only once after that.

Before he left me for the sea, Jack let me know by letter that he knew William was in love with me. He wrote:—

Cat,
Will's heart is yours for the taking, and you'd be a fool not to
hold on to it. He can, and will, give you everything I cannot.
As a true friend to you both, the best I can do is to accept this
commission in Alaska, where obligation awaits me. I would be
lying if I did not admit that my own heart is as equally
involved in its affection for you, and I fear if I stay, it would
only refuse to remain in the background.

Jack

Frances

If ten more guests were seated at this dinner table it could not be any noisier, nor could my temples be throbbing any harder than they are. Edward, son of my late brother, is my only living relative. He and his exasperating wife, Blanche, have invited me to share Thanksgiving with them. Regrettably I have accepted.

No fault can be found with the table their housemaid has laid, for she has seen to every last detail. Neither, apparently, has any expense been spared for a meal Edward's wife took no part in preparing. Blanche, who is as pale and drawn as her name implies, is too prodigal to realize that less is more; and that given the chance, I would trade my place at this flawless banquet for one of Catherine McFarley's simple, understated holiday meals in her family's humble parish home.

A carved roast turkey, accompanied by a dizzying selection of side dishes, have all been passed around the table, but the portions taken have barely made a dent in any of them. Heavy sterling forks and knives clatter against bone china while three of us volley for conversation that crisscrosses the dinner table as quickly as sputtering gunfire.

Two chilled bottles of Corton-Charlemagne Chardonnay, a 1925 Chateau Brane-Canenae Margaux, plus an additional sweet dessert sherry from Spain, is an overabundance of alcohol for any occasion where so few are dining. Such show of extravagance is appalling, even by my standards. Our country is still licking its wounds from the Great Depression, only to be followed by our involvement in an impending war with Europe. If my nephew and his frivolous wife thought to impress me with a meal that could have fed many less fortunate mouths, they have only succeeded in winning my disfavor.

"Auntie, won't you have more of something?" Edward invites. "Perhaps you'd like another slice of breast meat, or some sweet yams? The haricots verts are thin, just the way you like them."

"Good gracious, no!" I exclaim, pushing my plate away and pressing my hand to my chest. "Whoever did you think was going to eat all this food? We are but four, counting Mildred. The leftovers will spoil before they can be used."

"Why, I say there can be nothing but the best Thanksgiving feast for my Auntie Frances!" Edward guffaws, somewhat incoherently.

Since the start of the meal, I have watched him wash down nearly every mouthful of food with a swallow of wine. The buttons on his vest are already pulling too tightly.

"It is excess, Edward."

"Blanche would not have a holiday any other way than *full regalia*, Auntie, even with just the two of us here to partake of it."

"Well, I would say then that you have both wasted time and money. At my age, I am far easier to please and would have been just as satisfied with lesser fare. It would speak well of you both if you packed up some of these leftovers and shared them with those less fortunate. If Mildred calls your church, I am sure they can have the names and addresses of families who have nothing to eat today, much less a beautiful banquet as fine as this. Surely, this amount of food could feed at least ten hungry mouths."

Blanche's eyes narrow as she addresses me. "And who do you propose to deliver it? Do you suggest Edward leave us to cart food to those less fortunate?" Without moving her head, her eyes dart once at her husband and back again. "I believe your aunt would have been just as pleased with a roast capon and a few boiled potatoes."

"I can recall when it took far less to please you, Edward," I say, pretending his wife had not spoken. "Your mother was a simple cook. She was not one to waste so much as a nickel of your father's hard-earned wages. I should think that your parents, if they were here, would not only disapprove of your frivolous lifestyle in such strained economic times, but that they would be shocked by it."

I assume Blanch is draining her wine glass as a means of settling her nerves. She sets the crystal goblet firmly on the table, an imprint of her crass red lipstick marking its rim.

"Edward's tastes were abominable when I met him. In fact, I would go so far as to say they were nothing short of embarrassing," she snickers. "Why, when I met Edward, he couldn't tell Waterford from jelly jar glass. I should think that you, of all people, would appreciate just how far your nephew has elevated himself since marrying me, not to mention how far he has risen in his banking career."

"Darling, I am sure Auntie is very much aware of it all," Edward replies, gently patting his wife's hand as if to relax her. "Anyone can see that I am a changed man since marrying you, and all for the better. Aunt Frances agrees. Don't you, Auntie?"

"You are changed all right, Edward. But I daresay hardly for the better. Neither marriage nor success becomes you, though you and your wife may well think it does. Plainly put, you are on the verge of becoming a pompous bore." I add as an afterthought, "Perhaps Blanche finds that to be an attractive trait in a husband; however, I, for one, find it utterly and positively regrettable. I truly do."

The indignation on Blanche's face is so palpable, her color so high, I fear the dinner table might at any moment lift off the floor and levitate in midair. I look back at my nephew, whose mouth has remained open, and attempt to soften my tone.

"Why do you look so surprised, Edward? I am merely saying that you have changed, but that I very much enjoyed—alas, prefer—the former version of you. Your parents raised you with simpler values than those you are living by now, and I am relatively certain that both your father *and* your mother knew well the difference between crystal and jelly jars."

At this last barb, Blanche picks up the silver dinner bell and shakes it longer and harder than is warranted to bring Mildred scurrying from her post in the kitchen.

"We are done here, Mildred," she announces. Please serve dessert in the parlor, and I should prefer tea rather than port."

"All the more for us, Auntie," Edward tragically sports in an attempt to lighten the mood, but his wife glares at him.

Edward rises heavily, moving away from the table and crossing the room to the sideboard, where he pours each of us a thimbleful of the vintage dessert wine in delicate aperitif glasses. "It's the perfect accompaniment to Mildred's mince pie," he says lightly, passing the drinks to us as if they are peace offerings. Blanche declines with a wave of her hand.

"He is right, Blanche," I say, accepting the drink and taking a sip, then pressing my cloth napkin to stifle a burp. "A bit of port might do you some good. You look as though something has soured your stomach. My Bentley always said a 'bit of the grape' is not only good for digestion, but it also lifts the spirit and releases inhibitions. Personally, I have always been able to accomplish both with just a simple glass of water."

"You are naturally cheerful, Aunt," Edward states, still bent on flattery. "I have always thought it to be one of your most admirable traits."

With that, Blanche excuses herself, popping up from her chair as if it has caught fire. She exits the room silently, leaving a draft of hostility in her wake. If the moment is awkward, Edward is the only one feeling it. Personally, I am relieved for the chance to digest my meal without any further aggravation.

"I believe you have upset my wife, Auntie," Edward says, his words nearly inaudible.

"Forgive me, Edward, it was not my intention," I say, in my defense.

"Nevertheless," he replies, "I can tell she feels stung."

Edward casts a soulful expression my way, and I meet it squarely. I search for a fleeting glimpse of the thoughtful boy he used to be, the one I loved so dearly and treasured as though he were my own. Without Blanche to cloud my vision, I can now clearly see the man I was hoping to find.

"Oh, all right," I concede. "It was rude of me to goad Blanche. Let me enjoy the silence for just a moment more while we sip this superb port you have poured us, after which I shall go inside and make my apologies." I notice him visually relax. "But Edward, you must promise that you will try not to lose yourself in Blanche's quest to mold you into her version of who she thinks you should be. If it is Boston's society she is looking to impress, I can tell you those people are not worth it. Blanche may think that generosity and indulgence are noble qualities in a husband, but those attributes would be put to far better use by helping those less fortunate than you and your wife."

"Surely you are not faulting me for trying to secure a financial future for us and the family we one day hope to have?" Edward asks. "Blanche would see me broke before she would sacrifice a penny to charity when soon we will have children to provide for." He delivers a crooked smile, his blue eyes twinkling just as his father's used to. "Tell me," Edward asks, changing the subject, "which pie do you prefer—mince or pumpkin? Mildred has baked both for us, and I can smell them from in here."

Because he is king of his castle and I merely a guest in it, I allow my nephew to commandeer me from the dining room to their ostentatious parlor, where his wife is ensconced in a chair, like royalty, awaiting us. Blanche sits in stony silence, sipping tea which has been served from an ornate silver tea service set before her.

Edward clucks around me like a mother hen, settling me in a wingchair beside the fire and leaning my crutches against it. He removes a brass poker from beside the hearth and stabs mindlessly at the red hot embers before settling himself on the settee beside his wife.

It is because I spent so many years in my own dysfunctional marriage that I can so easily identify awkward imbalance when I see it. Here we sit, in our absurd family circle of three, with only the permeating aromas of Mildred's heated pies to lend any substance to the spirit of this holiday we call Thanksgiving.

I have observed an abrupt change in Edward's body language since coming into this room. He lights a cigarette and shifts uncomfortably in his seat, squaring his shoulders and seeming to brace himself for a possible confrontation, which may erupt in the event Blanche refuses to accept my forthcoming apology.

It is a disappointment to my heart that my nephew, once such a fun-loving and easygoing lad, has clearly been emasculated by a marriage vow. Looking at him now, I have every reason to believe that my little speech of a few minutes ago, no matter how well intended, has fallen on deaf ears.

Catherine

Though it is unseasonably warm for this time of year, a walk on the beach is customary on the Cape, even in winter. The sky, with its vast formations of cumulus clouds, could move even the most solemn of hearts on this spectacular November day, and I am counting on just such an inducement to work its magic for me while I contemplate telling William about Jack's letter.

William and I often bring Lizzie to the beach to expend her energy in hopes she will sleep through the night rather than wander into our bedroom in the wee hours as has been her bad habit of late. We stroll along, with Lizzie continually pulling her hand from the reassurance of ours. She runs ahead, her head bent halfway to her knees, weaving like a bloodhound, in search of artful scraps to add to an already overflowing, odoriferous collection of shells and other lifeless sea creatures stashed away in an old shoebox in the bottom of her closet. Fairylike, she dances away on tiptoes, her pink feet and long tanned legs poking out from beneath a dotted pinafore to tease the long foaming fingers of tide that eddy in and out of a languid bay.

William finds this particular stretch of secluded shoreline conducive to meditation, a blank canvas on which to create a sermon his parishioners can relate to. As we meander along in the wake of Lizzie's path to discovery, I cannot help but wonder if, when William looks out to sea, he ever thinks about the good times we shared with Jack long ago—when the three of us were young and our days carefree.

Long before Jack wrote of his coming home, I dreamed of it, longed for it. In dreams I see his ship, at first a microscopic dot on the horizon, becoming ever larger as my beckoning heart calls it home.

Unsure of how to broach the subject of Jack's letter, I flounder for an opening sentence. A convincing one fails to come to mind, so I ease into it by taking William's hand. He welcomes the gesture, giving my cool fingers a tender chafing to warm them. This insignificant sign of affection is enough to give me the courage I need.

"Jack Wakefield has written," I say as nonchalantly as I can muster.

Except for the flicker of a muscle in his lower jaw, William's expression is unflinching, but he releases my hand. This undoubtedly means that he is put off by the announcement.

"When did he write?"

"A couple of weeks ago," I lie, knowing full well the letter is two months old. I am surprised William's first question is *when,* rather than *why* and display a sign of good faith by volunteering the answer to what will undoubtedly be his next question. "He wishes to meet Jonah."

My husband's eyes grow dark, and I see the light fade from them, killing any good mood between us. "He writes *now*, after all this time? Why now? Why didn't you tell me right away?"

"I'm sorry. I apologize for not telling you sooner, but you've been so busy. Jack is determined to come. In fact, he was sailing from Alaska the very day he sent the letter. It's too late for any controversy from us."

I can tell he is trying to calculate how long it will take Jack to make the voyage. A look of total mistrust creases his handsome features, and I hasten my rambling.

"Apparently he is working on a trading vessel delegated to bringing mining supplies through the Panama Canal," I tell him. "Once there, he and a couple of crew members plan to rent a fishing boat and sail on to Cape Cod. He estimates their arrival to be sometime late September."

Lizzie has worked her way back to us. Proudly, she offers up her newly-found prize. This time it is a sundried horseshoe crab, its tail harpooned through a rusty can. "Look at what I found!" she exclaims with pride. "Isn't it super keen? I want to keep it."

"No, Lizzie, you can't. It's rusty, and it smells," her father says, prying the dehydrated fossil from her sandy hands while she argues with him.

Handing the crab to me to dispose of, William says under his breath, "We will continue this conversation later," and turns his back on me.

"I'll race you," he challenges Lizzie, who takes advantage of the head start he's giving her. "Dispose of that," he points with his chin and takes off, leaving me holding the rancid crab and no trash receptacle in sight.

Later that night, a storm makes landfall on the Cape. William, who has secured the window latches and brought in tomorrow's wood, is late coming to bed. I wait with trepidation for him to come to me thinking we might finish our conversation from the afternoon. It is my hope that the restricted space of our narrow bed may be advantageous in bringing about a peaceful resolve.

When he finally enters the room, he walks to his side of the bed and turns out the light. I feel him fold back his share of the covers, the familiar compression of mattress giving under his weight as he sits wearily on the edge of it. He does not turn but remains with the broad of his back facing me and says:—

"We...rather *you*, must tell Jonah soon; I won't have you putting it off."

"Fine," I say. "I will tell him tomorrow."

"What will you say?" he says coarsely, twisting his body to face me in the dark. "I'd like to know just how you intend to explain yourself to our son."

A heavy sigh escapes me. I have no clue how to tell Jonah that the man he has believed to be his father is really not. "I will have to think of a way," is all I say.

There is a moment's silence before William stands and fumbles inside the drawer of his nightstand. I hear him locate the box of wooden matches we keep there. There is the flick of the match head being struck across the side of the box. Light appears as the phosphorous tip of the match sparks and flares into flame. William bends and puts the flame to the candle wick.

Instantly, my husband's sour expression is illuminated. It appears before me as equally disturbing as the wafting smell of sulfur in my nostrils. Contradictory to his bad mood is the ambience of our bedroom, pleasantly transformed by a single lighted candle.

Perhaps it is only imaginary, but William's expression appears softened beneath the rosy hue, and my assumption is that he has lit the candle for its usual purpose—to enlighten our lovemaking. *Could this be his way of saying he understands about Jack and his ill-timed letter?*

I open my arms, and my husband comes to me. He bends his face to mine, his lips harshly demanding. Absent are the usual endearments he always murmurs at moments such as this; so taken aback am I by this unfamiliar approach to our lovemaking, I mistake it for ardor, attempting to raise my own passion to equal that of his.

William's response is anything but gentle or passionate. He bites my lips cruelly until I believe I can taste my own blood. An angry squeal of pain catches in my throat and tries to escape on an exhale of breath I cannot release.

I wrestle in his grip, fuming at his bullish aggression, but William's free hand holds the hair on the back of my head so firmly, I can barely move nor breathe. Our faces are pressed together so tightly, it feels as though we are sharing but one mouth, and I can do little more than whimper.

In one motion, William pushes my body flat to the mattress, working one of his knees between mine to pry them apart. For a moment our lips break contact. In our struggle, I raise an open hand to deliver a somewhat clumsy slap across his face.

"For God's sake, William, stop this!" I hiss, surprised to see a red welt blooming on his cheek.

The slap has brought him around. William stares blankly at me; the madness I had seen in his eyes a moment ago, gone.

"Catherine, forgive me!" he whispers, lifting himself off me to fall heavily onto his back. He covers his face with both hands; his rumpled hair damp with sweat and his rapid breathing slow to subside. Angrily, I wipe a finger across my lip and see it come away with a light smearing of blood.

"What has gotten into you?" I demand, already unwilling to accept any answer he could possibly offer.

"I don't know! I swear, I don't know! All these years, I've tried to shut him out," William cries, bolting from the bed. "Do you think I don't know that you think about him? That you miss him? The way he could make you laugh? How when we were growing up, he acted as if he could wrap the entire Cape, like a present with a bow to put in your hands? You think I don't remember all that?"

A drum roll of thunder rumbles somewhere far off in the distance; the storm has come and gone. With intermezzo strobes of lightning, the rumbling provides the background music to William's plight of threatened virility by a ghost from his childhood. His forlorn expression evokes sympathy in me, yet I cannot bring myself to reach out to him.

"Every time we make love—every time I set eyes on Jonah, I see *him!* Where the hell was Jack Wakefield all the time I've been raising his son? Seventeen years he's been gone, for God's sake!"

40

He rises up and comes around to my side of the bed where I lie, bewildered, cringing from the query of a man I thought I knew.

"Please don't look at me like that, Catherine—-I can't bear it!" He takes hold of my shoulders, giving them a little shake. "Tell me I'm wrong. Tell me that you don't think of him when we make love. Tell me," he pleads, shaking me harder this time, as though I am a rag doll to be tossed about.

"William, stop!" I demand. "You're hurting me!"

He relents, and I reach up to carefully release his grip from my shoulders.

"You are over-tired, William. Please, just come to bed. Let's try to sleep. We can deal with this tomorrow."

I move over, and William slides in under the covers, rolling toward me like a child, wanting me to cradle him in my arms. We remain this way, with William's head on my breast, while I soothe him by running my fingers through his hair. Finally, thankfully, he sleeps.

The storm moves further away, its echoed rumblings like distant drums in the night. If I were not guilty of infidelity in my mind; if William were not right in his every accusation, I could swear tonight's incident would never have occurred. But resentfully I move a fingertip over my bruised lip, realizing with certainty that it has.

What portion of blame is mine? I wonder. Is it possible after tonight for us to resurrect the love that has sustained us all these years?

It is our love, William's and mine, that I believe keeps Jonah secure. That same love rewarded us with Lizzie, the child of our own making. We are blessed. And we are damned.

In the dim of candlelight I feel very much alone, the thought of reconciliation a lonely and troublesome idea to ponder. The need to be comforted is suddenly so overwhelming, so primal, I feel all but consumed by it.

Carefully, I maneuver William's head from my chest so I might lean over his chest to blow out the candle and remain draped there, my own torso rising and lowering with the rhythm of his slumber.

Even in the dark, I can see the translucent veil of smoke spiral up off the expired wick, still glowing red-hot at its tip. The gossamer stream trails over my face like incense; the smell of molten wax, reminiscent of church, makes me believe that sleep will eventually come to me, even if dawn is riding on its heel.

I have little choice tonight but to befriend my sleeplessness. I let it enfold my infidel heart and transport it, on the wings of a trail of smoke, back in time...to Jack, and to the refuge of his safekeeping.

Jonah

My sister has caught a cold. Her nose has some nasty-looking stuff running out of it. She looks so pathetic I've agreed to sit beside her on the couch while she listens to *Little Orphan Annie* on the radio.

I make us two cups of Ovaltine, and together we listen to the chatty voice of Shirley Bell, who has been playing the role since she was ten. She's now roughly seventeen—the same age as me—and she's a star! Everyone knows that Annie's adventures are always shared with her trusted dog, Sandy, whose faithful bark goes, *Arf!*

Pretending she is Annie, Lizzie begs me to take on the role of the dog. I feel like a fool, but I get down on all fours. She loves it when I horse around with her.

That night, my parents wait until they are sure Lizzie is asleep before saying they need to speak to me in my father's study. Voluntarily entertaining my sister for the better part of the afternoon should have won me some points. I can't think of what I need to account for. Maybe one of them has found my Lucky Strikes. I'm sure the pack was there this morning, right where I keep them hidden, behind my stack of comic books. I'm sure I would have heard about it by now if my smokes had been discovered.

The long drapes in my father's study are drawn, making the room feel like a jail cell. Even the framed picture of The Sacred Heart, which has hung for years behind my father's desk, suddenly looks as though Jesus is trying to warn me with His woeful expression.

My parents enter the room together in silence. Father takes his usual seat behind his desk while Mother motions for me to sit beside her in one of the two chairs across from him.

What's going on? Mother is smiling a little, but she doesn't look happy. Father looks sad. Or does he just look serious? I'm not sure. My leg pumps nervously.

"It was good of you to play with your sister this afternoon the way you did, Jonah," Mother begins. "I think it made her feel better." She gives a weak smile and glances at my father as if she needs his permission to speak. "Have you ever heard us speak of our friend, Jack Wakefield?" she asks me.

So, I'm not in trouble after all. I relax my leg. "You mean the pirate fellow? Yes, I think so."

"He is a sailor—-a Captain, actually," Mother corrects me, as if the title makes any difference to me. Now she seems nervous. I see my father look away; I can't read his face.

"Captain Wakefield works for a trading company, based out of Alaska," Mother continues evenly. "Their ships deliver supplies to miners in those states that have mines and seaports, of course."

"Alaska. That's pretty keen," I reply, feeling myself relax even more.

Father has been quiet so far. He's just sitting there, looking serious. There is a stretch of silence, and then suddenly he speaks.

"Jonah, your mother and I have not called you in here to talk about Alaska. This is about Jack—or shall I say *Captain* Wakefield," he says flippantly. "It is about him...and you, son."

Wait. Me? I don't even know the guy.

Mother nervously continues:—

"You may remember, Jonah, in some of the stories I've told you about our childhood—your father's and mine—that all three of us were friends growing up?"

"You, dad, and this Jack fellow, right?"

"Yes, that is correct," Mother says, wringing her hands. "Well, you see, Captain Wakefield and I were at one point...more than just *friends.*"

I snicker. "Yeah, I think I get it. You mean like boyfriend and girlfriend."

"Yes, something like that," Mother replies, noticeably as uncomfortable as I'm beginning to feel. *I sure could use a cigarette right about now.*

"Your father and I think that you are now old enough to know the truth," Mother continues, clearly on the brink of tears.

What truth? Shit.

Mother, who is wearing a strand of pearls Father gave her, suddenly turns quiet. She rolls a single pearl between her fingers as if it is a bead on a rosary and she is praying with it.

"As you know, Jonah, sometimes people make mistakes. And sometimes...things happen due to those mistakes..." Unable to finish, she bursts into tears.

At first I just sit there. But when she doesn't stop crying, and father doesn't say or do anything, I jump up, nearly overturning my chair. I kneel down and wrap my arms around her. With her body folded inward she feels no bigger than my sister. Her wet tears soak through my shirt, and my own eyes well up to see her so distressed. A whiff of her hair fills the tiny space between us. It is an instinctual reminder of exactly who she is and of how much she means to me.

"Please, Mother," I beg, "please don't cry."

I turn to my father for help, but he has moved to stand by the window, looking out. I call out to him in a voice that quivers with concern, but he doesn't turn around. Then I notice his shoulders begin to heave with the weight of his own silent misery. And suddenly I am afraid.

Tears sting my eyes and threaten to spill over. "Will someone *please* just tell me what's going on?"

Mother lifts her head. "Jonah, what I have to say is going to come as a shock to you. I only hope it won't turn you against me."

"You're my mother," I tell her, "and I love you. Surely whatever you say could never change that."

"Go ahead, tell him," Father goads her. He is looking at Mother the way he looks at me when he expects a confession for something I've done wrong.

"Jonah," Mother gulps, "It's about Captain Wakefield..."

"Sure. What about him?" I ask.

"Jonah," Mother pauses. "Jack Wakefield... He is... You are—his son!"

What? What did she just say?

In an instant, Father is at my side. We are huddled together, all three of us equally upset, but I can't feel my father's arms, or his loving support.

I hear one of them cry, "My son! My poor boy!" But the voice is coming from very far away.

The room is spinning; the floor, falling. My name is being called over and over, but I can't find my voice.

And then, everything goes dark...

* * *

Father has never allowed me to play my trumpet in the house, even though I'm in my fifth year of lessons and can play fairly well. I have to go to the beach with my horn and stand on top of the dunes. Up there I fill my lungs with air, purse my lips to the small cup-shape opening of the mouthpiece, and *blow!*

The high, clear blast from the trumpet's bell never fails to send peaceful beach gulls into frantic flight, squawking and scattering in a million directions. Whenever I blow my horn up there on the dunes, I feel as free as those birds. The only other time I ever feel that liberated is when I'm standing near the sea. I never understood why that is—until now.

Lately, I've been going to the dunes with my trumpet. I play as long as my spare time allows—plaintive notes that come up from my very soul. I just blow that horn till there's nothing left in me to give. And sometimes in the evening, if the wind is at my back, I pretend it can carry my tunes across the sea—all the way across the states—from here on Cape Cod right on up to Alaska.

Frances

Dear Aunt Frances,
   Roses are red, violets are blue—
   We are expecting a baby,
   (To be named after you!)
      Love,
         Edward & Blanche

Of all the ridiculous announcements! I suppose I should feel flattered; for be it a boy or a girl, when the baby is born my name can be spelled as to accommodate either gender. Still, the parents-to-be are so affected and self-centered that I cannot comprehend how any offspring they produce could possibly stand a fair chance at a felicitous childhood. There is no doubt in my mind that, as the child's only great-aunt, I will have to bear the immense and burdensome responsibility to see that he or she is raised with some semblance of normalcy.

Edward has enclosed a note, penned on quality stock. He assures me that business has been profitable of late; that his company in Boston has agreed to cargo more automobiles to the Cape, resulting in a raise in salary beyond his expectations. His attempt at humor is to inform me that his wife is spending his paychecks faster than the ink used to sign them can dry. At this wit I smile mirthlessly, convinced his jest has more than a ring of truth to it. When I compare my nephew's marriage to Blanche to that of mine and his Uncle Bentley, I am hard pressed to find any good in it, for I see Blanche as nothing more than a shrewd opportunist, and my nephew the fool who gives in to her every whim.

Unlike their marriage, Bentley's and mine was one of convenience, enforced by two sets of parents at a time in our lives when we were too young to follow the direction of our own hearts. My southern-based parents knew that the Gellermont name would guarantee their crippled daughter an elevated acceptance among New England's society, while Bentley's convinced him that marrying a Wallingford would ensure him a monetary cushion far larger than the one his father had long ago gambled away.

The dowry I brought to the table was a sizable fiduciary, secure enough to withstand even the Great Depression. Once the knot had been tied, so to speak, Bentley Gellermont began drawing funds from what he perceived to be a bottomless pit. From the moment our vows were exchanged I had to endure, at my own (inherited) expense, my husband's portrayal of the benevolent benefactor.

We would never know the delirium of true love, Bentley and I, for Bentley was a philanderer, known for running his hands up every skirt available to him during our thirty-year marriage. He would often come home to our bed after a night of gaiety, reeking of liquor and another woman's perfume. Truth be told, I never loved Bentley romantically, and I suspect that it was his knowing this that in part drove him to his infidelities.

In all fairness, I was not without my own idiosyncrasies; and although my husband tried, he could not satisfy my carnal longings. Masculine ardor and the advances that ensue have never held an appeal for me. Therefore, I was secretly relieved on those nights when Bentley elected to sleep elsewhere. We learned to live within the boundaries of a mutual marital understanding, which resulted in our cohabitating together quite amicably. Eventually we chose to spend our *golden years* on Cape Cod. It was here on the Cape that Bentley and I enjoyed some of our best times together, until he died four years ago of congestive heart failure.

I am fifty-two years old, yet romantic love is still foreign to me. In addition to my age, widowhood has convinced me that such love will forever elude me. Still, there are times when I am in the company of my beloved friend, Catherine McFarley, laughing and sharing some tidbit of gossip, that I feel romance is still within my reach. When Catherine is asking if there is anything she can do to see to my comfort; when I am focused on her animated features and listening intently to her musings, it is then that I believe I have come as close to loving another human being as will ever be possible for me.

As a matter of routine, I feel for the pins that are securing my wool hat to my hair and adjust its tilt. Catherine is coming around with the car to take me to the dentist. I have a molar that has been causing me discomfort for some time now, and it is time to have the problem checked. After my appointment, I shall treat Catherine to lunch at that little sandwich shop in Orleans that she is so fond of.

My sable brown suit is much too formal for a trip to the dentist and a meager lunch, but it seems my wardrobe has always been too fine for the likes of New Englanders, or far too impractical for seashore dwelling.

I think back to when Bentley and I lived in Manhattan and how well dressed we always were then. It was easy for Bentley to be permissive with his spending—to lavish us both with *my* money. Many evenings passed without him being there with me, but Bentley always assumed his absences could be reconciled by the gifting of a fanciful chapeau or a costly fur from Lord & Taylor or Saks Fifth Avenue. I am not sure of which I was more resentful: the fact that Bentley imagined my forgiveness could be store-bought, or that some wretched animal had undoubtedly suffered so that some woman, such as I, could be futilely adorned in its fur.

Admittedly, I do adore fashion. If I thought for a minute she would go with me, I would book two tickets to Florida for Catherine and myself, upon the Southern Flyer, and I would purchase for us a few of those all-white dresses that have become all the rage. If only I were not encumbered by these dreadful crutches, or my friend by her commitment to family.

Always punctual, Catherine's gentle knock can be heard at the front door, and my housemaid drops what she is doing and hurries to answer it. She opens the door to reveal Catherine huddling behind it. Even from this distance, I recognize the look on my friend's face as one of grave concern. She steps forward to help take my handbag from me, tucking it under her arm, along with her own purse. As we head slowly for the door, she whispers low:—

"There is something I must speak to you about, Frances— something quite serious."

"What is it?" I ask, pivoting on my crutches and lending my full attention. "Shall I cancel my appointment? I could have Mary prepare lunch for us right here, if you would rather stay put."

"No, no, that is not necessary. Besides, I've been looking forward all week to having lunch with you. I will explain everything after we've eaten, though I'm afraid I've not got much of an appetite."

"Then we must be sure to keep it light and share only the best of gossip over lunch," I joke, but Catherine's mouth is set in a grim line.

I inch one crutch closer that I may take hold of my friend's hand. "Surely you know that you can tell me anything, Cat. I will always keep to myself anything you ever confide in me and will never pass judgment on you."

"I know that, Frances, which is one of the reasons you are so very dear to me."

"Let's not leave the house with this heavy burden on your shoulders," I urge, still holding her hand. "At least tell me what this is about."

Catherine hesitates a moment, looking past my shoulder to make sure Mary is not within earshot. She drops her voice. "It's about Jack Wakefield."

"Jack Wakefield!" I say, my eyebrows lifting with surprise. "Now there's a name I haven't heard mentioned for years. Has anyone even heard from that scallywag in all this time?"

"Yes," Catherine answers, sighing heavily and letting her hand slip from mine, "I have."

Catherine

Across my lap lies a weighty atlas. I have brought Lizzie here to the library for a children's arts and crafts project. Whatever paper and paste creations the children are making downstairs are for family Christmas gifts, which every parent will treasure no matter what it looks like nor how clumsily it has been put together.

If I had thought it through I could have left Lizzie here, for the group is well supervised, and gone to do some much-needed Christmas shopping. There is but little to spare in our personal account and, as usual, the burden falls on me to stretch it far enough so that our children receive at least one thing that they are wishing for. But instead of making efficient use of my free time, I am researching sea passages from Alaska to New England. *God help me for the wretch I've become since Jack wrote of his coming!*

Every day I read articles in the local paper about that madman, Adolf Hitler, with his obsessive declaration to ultimately conquer Europe, and shudder to imagine another world war. It may very well come to that, but the universal meaning of Christmas will, at least for this month, override any grim prospect by its eternal message of joy and peace on earth—that and Jack's return.

Just the thought of Jack's face when he finally sets eyes on Jonah is Christmas gift enough for me. The decadent, forbidden fruit of his anticipated visit has me acting as flighty and frivolous as Elizabeth can be. I find myself desiring time to fly by, even though Jack's troublesome letter has caused an irrevocable rift in my marriage. Our household will never be the same now that Jonah knows the truth.

To complicate matters, Frances has taken a pre-empted stand against Jack's visit, coming to William's defense every time I so much as broach the subject with her. When she stands on that moralistic soapbox of hers, I inevitably come away feeling every bit the whore, tearfully defensive about the desires of my youth, my brazen behavior sixteen years ago.

For now I sit here exploring waterways—trusting that some spiritual light, some beacon of hope will guide my fragile marriage through the test of endurance. I fear I am guilty of not giving enough thought or credit to my husband and all that he has been for me, for us.

Jonah's handsome features—his spindly boy-to-man physique, and probably his zest for life—Jack can take credit for. But the boy's genuine goodness, his humility and raw innocence—these qualities are the laborious results of William's nurturing. It takes a letter from Jack Wakefield to make me stop long enough to assess my husband, to see him for the man he is.

My not-so-revolutionary thoughts are interrupted when a woman next to me accidentally drops one of the books she has gathered in her arms. She stoops to retrieve it and I see it is the new novel, *Out of Africa,* by Isak Dinesen. Frances told me about it, humorously commenting on how the storyline reminded her of her own faithless marriage to Bentley. She had said the author is actually Baroness Karen von Blixen-Finecke, married to her cousin, the Baron himself, and that the story is her lyrical meditation of life on her coffee plantation in Nairobi.

Eager to read the written words of a woman so fiercely independent and capable, I set aside the atlas and walk over to the front desk to inquire whether another copy of the novel is readily available. I am told that it is. While I wait for it, the release of a heavy door being pushed opened shatters echoes down the hall.

The gaiety of twenty adolescents thunders throughout the tomb-like silence of the library's vaulted ceilings, each high-pitched voice volleying to be heard. Two somberly-dressed librarians slip out of nearby nooks to silence the group, holding their forefingers to their lips with a *sh-h-ush*-ing noise that sounds like steam escaping a radiator.

Elizabeth spots me at the front desk having my book stamped. She rushes to me with her bag of crafts, the metal buckles on her snow boots jingling like sleigh bells. She is wearing the same red wool coat and hat she has worn for the past two winters, and I take note that this must be her last year to wear it, for the cuffs are already a half inch too short.

Lizzie reaches into her pocket to pull out her woolen gloves, losing one to the floor. She stoops to retrieve it, and I have a nostalgic flashback of my attaching a small length of yarn to her mittens. I bend down and softly recite:—

"Little Kitten, you've dropped your mittens. Now you shall have no pie."

"I'm too old for nursery rhymes," my daughter reminds me, taking immediate inventory to make sure none of the other girls have overheard my quip.

"I suppose you are, but not too old to kiss, I hope." I quickly bend to bestow a peck of a kiss on a rounded pink cheek that feels as soft and warm as a firm summer peach against my lips.

"Do I have time to get a book, Mama?" Lizzie asks.

"Yes, so long as you do it quickly," I tell her.

She hands me her craft bag, making me swear I will not peek inside it. Thankfully, she does not dawdle but returns quickly with a copy of *Little Women*. I smile inwardly and stand aside so she may hand her selection to the librarian for stamping. The teetering balance between Elizabeth's rush to become a young woman is in contradiction with her ardent desire to remain a child; it makes my heart lurch to witness the graceful transformation.

One glance at the clock on the wall tells me that we're late. I've yet to stop at the butcher to buy something for tonight's dinner, plus I wanted to stop by the florist to order poinsettias for the church. If time after chores allows, I hope to check in on Frances, but that will depend on how fast I can get everything done.

I'm still at odds as to what to give her my best friend for Christmas. *What does one give to someone who has everything?* It must be something special—something to express my appreciation of her friendship. She was rather stoic when I told her about my past involvement with Jack Wakefield. She is a true friend, whose wise council keeps me on the straight and narrow path even when I find myself undecidedly at odds.

With our books and bag in hand, I hustle Lizzie out of the library and down the steps to our car, which luckily is parked nearby. A light, slick snow has begun to fall from a sky that looks unfavorably dark for so early in the day. Since there won't be time after stopping at the butcher's to go to both the florist and to see Frances, I must budget my time. Ordering flowers for the church is a necessary errand, whereby a visit with Frances is merely frivolous. If William were here he would advise me to choose the more important of the two.

It takes two seconds for me to decide to forgo the trip to the florist.

Jonah

"Jonah, I'll need you to take this tray to your father," Mother tells me, while she arranges two china cups with their saucers beside a matching tea pot that has a noticeable chip on its spout. She has brewed a full pot of tea using only one fresh tea bag plus a used one from this morning, which she had left to dry on the spoon rest on top of the stove. Re-using tea bags is just another attempt on her part to conserve during lean times. I admire that, even though that second cup of tea is always too weak for my liking.

She had put out a plate with two slices of crusty bread on it for my sister and me. Now she takes one of them, spreads a lick of strawberry jam on it, slices it in two and adds them to the tray.

"Why did you do that?" Lizzie asks. "We need two pieces."

"You two will have to share; we need one slice for our guest."

"Who is here?" Lizzie asks. "Can I go see who it is?"

"No, you may not," Mother says, adding a pitcher of cream, a small bowl of sugar cubes, and two cloth napkins to the tray.

Wiping her hands on her apron, Mother signals to me to take the tray to the study. Father is behind closed doors with Mr. Benjamin Fromlehide, the town's funeral director, or as I like to call him, *Old Formaldehyde*, probably come to discuss arrangements for a funeral service.

The teacups rattle on their saucers and a bit of cream sloshes over the rim of the pitcher as I step lightly from the kitchen and through the living room, crossing the hall to the study. I balance the tray on the small butler table outside the door and knock softly. The muffled conversation on the other side ceases momentarily. Father opens the door.

"Ah, tea has arrived!" he announces brightly, ushering me into the room, which suddenly smells like mothballs.

I can feel a pair of rheumy eyes assessing me as I bend to place the tray with unsteady hands upon the coffee table between father and his guest. When I straighten up, I cringe to see Old Formaldehyde still resembles Ichabod Crane, in *The Legend of Sleepy Hollow*. He is dressed in his customary black suit, his bony limbs protruding sharply at every joint. His pointy face is ashen (one would never guess he lived on the Cape), and his mouth is but a gash beneath a parrot-beak of a nose.

One skeletal hand rests on the knob of his silver-tipped cane while he extends the other, obviously waiting to be served. Nervously, I fill his cup and pass it to him, spilling some of the tea into the saucer in the process.

"Most kind of you, Jonah, thank you," the old man says, unsmiling. Before he takes a sip, he remarks:—

"Your father was just telling me about your ministry studies. So then, am I to understand that you plan to follow in your father's footsteps?"

Here is my chance, I think to myself, taking note of my father's confident expression, which says he is sure my answer will not let him down.

"Actually, no—sir," I reply, finding my nerve and hanging on to it. "I don't see myself as a minister."

From the corner of my eye, I catch a glimpse of my father's face. It is set as firmly as cement.

"Preposterous!" the old man sputters, nearly choking on his tea. Next to Father, Mr. Fromlehide's opinion is the second most sought after by people in this town. "And just what do you propose to do with yourself when you are finished with school, young man? Why, your Father is most respected! He is a minister's son himself, just as your grandfather was before him! It is only fitting that you should want to continue the generational lineage of spiritual vocation, and I should think you would be proud to do just that."

He glares at me from under bushy eyebrows that look like two caterpillars touching head-to-head. If I were not so nervous, I could laugh.

"It's only natural, I suppose, that Jonah should feel reluctant," Father says, offering me the chance to redeem myself. "After all, it is not an easy road this calling to serve God."

Like an owl on a limb, Mr. Fromlehide turns his head around nearly two-thirds and blinks at my father.

"What job *is* easy, William? Do you think *my* job is easy? I would tell you, sir, it definitely is not! Not only are jobs hard to come by, but they will be harder to come by as time goes on. Your son should not be misguided into thinking he can afford to be selective. In fact, if Jonah does not take a position with the church, the chances of his being called to serve his country in a war that is not ours to fight will be dramatically increased."

"If only I could be called, sir!" I blurt out, "I would be damn proud to serve America fight the Germans!" *I can't believe I just said that.*

I turn on my heels and leave the room, taking large strides, and half expecting to feel my father's hand restraining me by the collar, but he does not come before I'm able to grab my coat from the rack in the foyer and escape out the door.

Ever since that fateful night when I was told about my conception, the relationship between Father and me has been strained. I doubt what I just said about not wanting to be a minister comes as any revelation to him. Now that I know whose son I really am, I don't have to pretend anymore to be something or someone I don't wish to be. Thanks to old man Fromlehide's nosiness, my true feelings have been made known, and I am finally free to follow my own dream, not one that someone else dreams for me. I know for a fact that if I am to be true to myself and follow in my father's footsteps, at sea is where I belong.

Hunching my shoulders to my neck, I wish I had time to have grabbed a hat and some gloves before running out the door. I feel the burn of cold on my ears and try to cover them the best I can with my coat collar and shove my hands into the side pockets to try to keep warm, bracing myself against a frigid northeast wind as I head for the beach. Even in this weather, a deserted Cape beach, that secluded monastery of solace, is the only place I have ever found where I can actually be myself.

Frances

"**S**he looks like a clip joint moll," I remark in a stage whisper intended for Catherine's ear alone, while I eyeball Blanche in her flapper-style dress with its rebellious hemline. Seven of us have gathered around the Christmas tree for a boisterous gift exchange, which thankfully has finally ended. Praise the Lord.

"What's a *moll?*" Catherine asks, sipping from her glass of champagne.

"Heavens, Cat, you are an innocent! A *moll*—you know, a gangster's girl," I explain. "That dress is far too short for an expectant mother who has already begun to show."

Catherine shrugs. "It's Christmas. She probably wanted to look especially nice for the occasion."

"Bah, humbug!" I reply, peering over the arm of my wing chair at the stack of token gifts on the floor. "She does not look nice. She looks like a tart. Now you, on the other hand, look exceptionally smart in your elegant black wool skirt and flattering white blouse. Tell me, do you like my Christmas gift?"

"Oh, yes!" Catherine breathes, fondling the gold initial pin, with a miniature diamond at the base. "It's obscenely generous, Frances. You should have given this fine a gift to Blanche. She is, after all, family."

"I should absolutely *not* give her such a gift!" I retort, rapping my hand on the arm of my chair harder than intended and thereby drawing attention to myself.

I lean toward Catherine and lower my voice. "That woman is a gold digger if ever there was one! Why, when I die she and my nephew will have the very fillings from my teeth before my body's cold, mark my words!"

Catherine snorts lightly and covers her mouth, drawing further attention upon us.

"Blanche will be happy with the lace tablecloth I gave her or she can go home empty-handed," I say. "Either way, it won't matter a fig to me."

Catherine tilts her head and looks at me with a critical eye. "You sound rather like *Ebenezer Scrooge*."

"Bah, humbug!" I confirm and dismiss the subject of Blanche by smoothing the fabric of my Chanel suit across my lap.

I reach over to gently lift the fine deep-red wool shawl from where it is folded in the top box beside the chair.

"I simply adore this shawl you knit for me, Catherine," I say, fingering the soft fibers, "though how you managed to get your hands on wool so fine, I can't imagine. What did you have to do for it, sell your soul to the devil?"

"We both know that already happened years ago," Catherine jokes, but I find no humor in joking about having an illegitimate child—only shame.

Her joke falling short, Catherine rises to refill her glass of champagne, offering to top mine. "Let me have a closer look at the stationery Edward and Blanche gave you," she says.

I remove it from the stack of gifts beside my chair and hand it to her. The stunning blue box of *Crane* paper, with my name embossed in gold lettering, speaks well for my family's expensive taste. However, seeing as how money has always meant less to me than it ever has to them, my dear friend's hand-knit shawl, with its fine tight stitches, is by far my most cherished Christmas present this year.

"Very lovely," Catherine remarks, closing the box and handing it back to me. "I'm sure everyone, including myself, appreciates their gifts this year." Her eyes travel across the room and she points with her chin. "Will you just look at Elizabeth? She has not moved from that box of ballerina paper dolls since unwrapping them. And a diary with a lock and key—that may mean trouble! I can't remember when I last saw that child so entertained." She swivels in her seat to peruse the room. "I haven't seen Jonah, have you?"

I shake my head that I have not.

"His behavior is beginning to worry me," Catherine admits, absentmindedly nibbling a fingernail.

"Why? Have you noticed a difference in him since you told him about Jack?"

"Yes. He's been rather sullen at home. It seems that new friend of his, Rachel Coulter, is the only one he opens up to anymore."

"It's only natural he's pulled away a bit. After all, he has suffered a shock, learning about Jack the way he did. The girl is his age, someone he can easily relate to."

"True," Catherine agrees. "Still, I used to be the one he turned to when he had something on his mind."

"He's growing up. And I'm not surprised he is popular with girls. But you're his mother; he knows where you are if he needs you."

"Perhaps he's gone outdoors to try his new camera," Catherine guesses. "Really, Frances—imagine giving a teenager such a costly gift. I'll have one more thing to do making sure he takes proper care of it."

"Doesn't every boy Jonah's age own a Kodak Jiffy Six-20 camera?" I mock her. "In all seriousness, I felt it was important that Jonah be made extra happy this year."

Catherine shoots me the same look she gives her children when they are pushing the limit.

"You are a spoiler of children, you are, and far too generous. None of us could ever begin to repay you."

"I ask for nothing in return but your friendship, which I know I've always had," I say. "Besides, Christmas is a time for giving, and I so enjoy doing just that."

I survey the room. The men are huddled in conversation, while across the room Blanche is near dozing. "Do you not think it rude of the men to hole up in a corner while we women are left to entertain ourselves? Why, Blanche is falling asleep from boredom."

"She's resting," Catherine observes. "She told me the pregnancy is taking it out of her."

"Taking what?" I ask, selecting a confection from the plate in front of me. "She does little to begin with." I pop a butter cream in my mouth and pass the plate to my friend.

Catherine gracefully changes the subject. "William was overjoyed with the brass desk lamp you gave him! If only I had thought to give him something as handsome instead of leather gloves."

"A useful gift and of very fine leather," I tell her, glancing William's way. "Your husband hasn't stopped preaching since he got here. He and Edward are still at it. I say, how boorish!" Gently, I manipulate a few frizzy curls at the nape of my neck, decidedly convinced that my last perm was rolled too tight. "Dare we interrupt them?"

There comes a draft as Jonah enters through the front door in the hallway, a gust of icy wind accompanying him into the house. Elizabeth authoritive tone can be heard questioning her brother as to his whereabouts. I see a flash of light and hear the *pop* of an expired flashcube. Elizabeth shouts, and Jonah laughs maliciously.

"I can't see!" Elizabeth cries, stumbling into the room to find her mother. Jonah saunters in behind his sister, the camera dangling from the strap around his neck.

Blanche rises from the settee and moves to the gramophone to replace the sedate Christmas carols I had selected with a recording by Django Reinhardt, better known as *The Sultan of Swing*. Balancing her glass in one hand and a long cigarette holder in the other, Blanche begins moving her hips to the catchy tempo of *I'se A Muggin'*.

"Wanna dance?" she asks Jonah, dipping her chin and all but batting her eyes at him.

"If you tip your soda or drop a hot ash on my Persian carpet, Blanche, you're going to rue the day!" I say, pulling her attention away from the boy.

Catherine, who has been straightening up around the room and tossing wrapping paper and ribbon into the fire is oblivious of Blanche's blatant flirting, but at least her movement about the room is enough to catch her husband's attention from where it has been for most of the afternoon.

William's face takes on a devilish appeal as he rises from his seat and motions to all of us not to give him away. This is a side of him none of us has ever seen. Catherine is taken by surprise when William sneaks up behind her, grabs her by her waist, and sweeps her off her feet.

Catherine shrieks, the wrinkled gift wrap she's been gathering floating through the air as William swings her thrice around in a full circle. Both of them are dizzy and laughing like children when William carefully places his wife on her feet and then leans in for a kiss. It is as romantic a moment as any, and I feel the frozen smile harden on my face, followed by a cold stab of jealousy.

Edward, who up to now had been unsociable, calls to me from across the room. "Aunt Frances, what do you say we *cut the rug* with a little *rag?* Let's show these people how to really get this party going!"

I put my hand up to protest, but Edward is already guiding me out of my chair with two strong arms.

"I need my crutches, Edward!"

"Trust me," he says, "I'll not let you fall."

He smells rather handsomely of leather and pipe tobacco. He takes my hand in his and positions his other around my matronly waist. I feel him pull me tightly to him, securing me snugly against his sturdy frame until we are balanced.

Blanche has changed the record again, this time to a recording of waltz tunes. I groan, insisting that I am too encumbered for such frivolity, but Edward's slow, gliding foot movement is a festive reminder to me of days gone by.

My body relaxes, and we move in unison, as I allow my nephew to move me along. Not since Bentley have I danced in the arms of such an attractive man. I close my eyes. The year is 1893, and I am dancing with my dear departed brother, Henry.

Henry is twelve years old and I have just turned eight. We are dance partners at our parents' holiday soirée, held each year in our New York penthouse. I'm wearing a fine dress of crimson velvet, the hemline of which is almost long enough to hide my metal leg braces. On my feet is a new pair of shiny black patent leather shoes. Henry is holding me so that my two feet are atop his, synchronized to move when he does. We manage our little stilted waltz, my older brother and I, rounding and circling the room like a spinning top gathering momentum. Guests applaud and our parents wave to us as we pass them by. My braces are nowhere to be seen, but I have no need of them while my brother holds me like this. And we dance...

"Hold it!" Jonah calls out, holding his new camera up to one eye.

Cheek to cheek, Edward and I raise our heads and look into the camera. We hear, "Smile!" And a flash bulb bursts into blinding light.

My guests applaud, and I am overcome to be surrounded this Christmas by those nearest and dearest to me. Whatever obstacles any of us are experiencing—be it hard times or the impending threat of war—at this moment there is only joy in the room, and it is a good and tangible thing.

Catherine

It was naïve of me to think that William and I could make a fresh start with the New Year. The damp, dank days of winter have only just begun, and there is nothing less savory than the Cape in winter time. Oddly enough, William revels in it. He holes himself up in his study and spends hour upon hour reading scripture and writing sermons.

Our house is only warm when the sun is out. Most days we suffer what seems to be the infinite sogginess that chills one to the bone. Any stray pieces of wood found lying outside, be it scrub pine or oak, one of us carries in to save for the night's fire. Even Lizzie knows to replenish the stash and will enter the house from time to time with an armful of spindly twigs to add to the kindling box beside the hearth.

Only on those nights that call for it, William will light a fire for us and don a sweater before retreating to the temperate seclusion of his study. There he composes sermons riddled with consternation for the world's state of affairs and warns his parishioners that repentance paved with loving example is the only road to salvation. As cerebral as my husband is, he is allowing life to pass him by, which I believe is ultimately making both of us old and stodgy before our time. I look and feel very much the old woman, mending socks by the light of the fire and a floor lamp in an otherwise darkened parlor.

Our son is outside sledding with friends, though I would venture to guess that tonight the blades of his sled must rely on slush for traction rather than snow. There has been little in the way of snow accumulation around these parts, certainly not enough to sled on.

I wonder if that new girl, Rachel Coulter, is with him. When she and her family first came to town, Jonah began talking about the interesting girl he was sharing science class with. He told us her parents are weather experts of some sort and that Rachel's father has a PhD in meteorology. How a degree in meteorology feeds a family today, I cannot fathom. Even more perplexing is why the Coulters, who come from Florida, have chosen the Cape and Rhode Island as prime locations for studying weather conditions. After all, everyone knows that the seasons across the eastern seaboard are fairly predictable, with the exception of an occasional nor'easter.

Jonah makes fun of his new friend and her bohemian parents, saying they are *off the cob,* which means *corny.* But I think our Jonah, who has begun spending a fair amount of time in the Coulters' scientific habitat, eating unhealthy meals while discussing climatology and weather-related jargon, has taken a shine to this odd little kewpie doll, Rachel Coulter. I'm sure I am right. Mothers have a sixth sense about things like this.

Jonah may be drifting away from me in his quest to become a man, but Lizzie is still mine—at least for the time being. Presently she is sprawled on the floor in front of a fire that is waning, her hair damp from her bath but shining under the glow of the lamp. This is one of those moments that permanently imprint themselves, like photographs, in the scrapbook of a mother's heart. My little girl, looking deceitfully angelic in her favorite soft flannel nightgown with its rosebud pattern, is fresh from the tub and smelling of Ivory soap. Her head is bent so low over her homework, her nose is nearly touching the page, and there is a selection of school supplies splayed carelessly and colorfully within her reach.

The heat from the fire is making her drowsy; I can tell she is tempted to doze. If she didn't look so adorable, I'd be aggravated with her for waiting this late to complete her assignments.

An hour of sighing and changing positions has her head drooping languidly. At my urging, she gathers her belongings, stands up, and raises her arms over her head.

"Are you ready for bed?" I ask, laying aside a sock I've been mending and removing my spectacles that I might rub my own eyes.

"When is Jonah coming home?" Lizzie asks.

"He should be here any minute," I say, standing also to stretch and chafe my arms against the chill in the room, wishing we could purchase a coal stove soon.

I pick up the poker and stoke the red-hot embers, toss another few pieces of dry wood on top of them and watch the flames take hold. They lick at the parched bark hungrily— crackling and dancing, their intensely blue centers eventually biting into the dehydrated log.

William enters the room, bleary-eyed. He places both hands in the small of his back and leans from side to side. "Have we any tea? I need to take a break."

"Yes, of course," I say, touching his arm. "I'll put the kettle on and join you."

He looks at Lizzie and cocks his head indulgently. "Are you just now finishing your lessons? I would have thought you were long done."

"I didn't have much," Lizzie says, wrapping her flannel-clad arms around her father's neck to bury her nose under his jaw. "Stoke the fire, please, Father, or I'll freeze in my bed tonight."

"I will, but you must hurry along now. You don't get enough sleep as it is, and then you refuse to get up in the morning when it is time to."

While he is seeing Lizzie to bed, I carry two steaming cups of tea to the study and set them upon William's desk, in the only fraction of clearing that I can see. Today's copy of the Cape Cod Standard-Times is on the corner of the desk. Fragments of pipe tobacco fall to the floor as I pick up the paper glance briefly at an article about the Works Progress Administration. Their latest expansion into large arts, drama, and literacy projects is encouraging. President Roosevelt, with his ambition to help the country rebuild with organizations such as the WPA and the Civilian Conservation Corps, is a glimmer of hope for us all at the end of what has been a very dark tunnel.

Any attempt to organize my husband's desk would confuse him, so I replace the paper where I found it and bend my head at to read a portion of scripture from what I believe is Proverb 4:18, Verse 4:

> *Do not set foot on the path of the wicked*
> *or walk in the way of evil men.*
> *Avoid it, do not travel on it:*
> *turn from it and go on your way.*
> *For they cannot sleep till they do evil:*

they are robbed of slumber till they
make someone fall.
They eat the bread of wickedness
and drink the wine of violence.

William has entered the room as stealthily as a cat, making his presence known with his warm breath stirring the fine hairs on my neck as he peers over my shoulder. I turn to him, my expression set so he won't read the dismay in my eyes. I fear that the expectation of Jack's trip home has affected my husband's reasoning. Short of the unavoidable voyage being cancelled, I wish he could understand that I am not at fault and therefore am powerless to set William's mind on a more secure footing.

"What do you think?" he asks, lifting the teacup to his lips and taking a long draught.

No doubt he wonders whether or not I have caught the underlying meaning of the passage he's chosen. However, I usually know when I am being provoked—most specifically, by my husband. I shrug, careful to appear innocent in my assessment. Taking two delicate sips of my own tea, I measure his mood before answering:—

"Only that it is possibly too weighty a message during these times when people are looking for a lift of spirit, especially just after the holiday season."

"On the contrary," William counters. He sets down his cup and comes to me. Seductively he twirls a tendril of my hair around his finger and drops a kiss, as light as a feather, upon my nape. "All of us need be reminded from time to time of the evil doings of those whose mission in life is to poison any good they happen upon and covet what is not theirs."

His meaning is crystal clear, but I play the naiveté and move beyond its implication.

"William, you are bound to lose popularity with the parishioners with this controversial way of thinking. People come to church to have their spirits uplifted, not to be put into decline."

"What is controversial about protecting what is one's own—that which is sacred to him or her?" he asks.

"There is a difference between protecting and unduly mistrusting," I say, turning to face him. "I see your shielding instincts as bordering on paranoia."

"Why? Because I don't want taken from me what is rightfully mine?" he asks, defensively.

"Surely you're not referring to Jonah," I say.

"You know that I am."

"And just who do you suspect is taking Jonah from you?" I prod, wishing I had thought to keep the news of Jack's letter to myself.

"Jack Wakefield—that cad! Can't you see it? For God's sake, Catherine, open your eyes. Jack wants our boy. Or did you think he was just going to stop off to say hello and then sail off again?" Struggling to keep his voice low, William's face creases deeply at the thought of losing the son he adores. It is a déjà vu moment for me as I visualize us in our bed that stormy night two months ago.

"Jack would never—could never—take Jonah from you, William. If he were standing here right this minute, even Jack would admit it is *you* who has been the true father to Jonah." I step closer to encircle his slender waist with my arms and bring them to rest naturally on his hips. "Jonah loves you," I say convincingly. "We, your family, love you—more than you could ever know."

A small cry escapes his lips as he drops his head on my shoulder and takes me in his arms to crush me against him. This simple gesture may be a means to measure the depth of his uncertainty, though why my husband sees himself as a lesser man than Jack Wakefield leaves me at a loss. Jack may have incomparable charm and can play a woman's body like a finely tuned instrument, but William has integrity and is honorable—-two qualities Jack has never possessed nor ever understood the meaning of.

We separate when we hear Jonah enter the house, our expressions changing favorably. Instinctively, we both glance at the grandfather clock against the wall to check it against our son's curfew. Jonah calls out a greeting from the stairwell and we hear the heavy thud of his feet going up the stairs.

William turns back to me and gives me a wry look that tells me the fight has gone out of him. Just as we always do when the children are present, we let it go.

"I should make sure his boots made it to the mat," I sigh, moving toward the door. "He is forever leaving them wherever he takes them off, and I don't want to have to mop the foyer before going to bed tonight. If the party line is not occupied, I should also ring Frances to make sure she is set for the night."

"Wait," William says, crossing the room to gently close the door. "You are extremely good to Frances, Cat—perhaps too much so." He takes his familiar repose behind his desk, and I realize he has more to say. "I believe your good friend to be far more capable than you allow her to be and in less need of the assistance you feel so obligated to provide for her. There is something about Frances that has always left me somewhat *reserved* in my opinion of her."

"What do you mean?"

"Let's just say that I think her affection for you is unnatural," he says. "Unconventional, if you will."

"William, I find that to be a cynical remark," I say, having been taken off-guard, "especially coming from a pastor. Frances is your most esteemed bene-factress. I am shocked; and frankly, rather appalled, that you would entertain such thoughts, much less express them verbally."

"My feelings have nothing to do with her money. Frances, and Bentley when he was alive, have always been most generous in their donations to the church. That, however, does not mean that we must be beholden to the Gellermonts. Intuitively I have felt this way about Frances for some time now—years, actually." He sits down and picks up his pen. "I should prefer that if you won't put some distance between yourself and Frances, that you at least heed my warning. Proceed with caution—and keep a wary eye out."

"Your accusation is ludicrous!" I exclaim, shaking my head in disbelief. But my voice comes out strained and it lacks conviction.

"I am not accusing her," William says.

"But you are! You believe the feelings of my dearest friend to be impure, and I refuse to believe that about Frances!"

"Even so, Cat," William replies evenly. "Despite your opposition, I must insist that you tread carefully."

Jonah

There's nothing like a dame to wash away the blues, and no dame quite like Rachel. She's standing in the doorway of her house, watching me step around wide puddles of street slush to get to her.

It wasn't easy getting out of bed this morning, it being a Saturday and all; but we agreed that if there's time after we finish our science assignment, I'd take her to the docks to watch the fishing boats come in.

"I didn't think you'd make it," Rachel greets me, looking like the bee's knees in a pair of wide-leg trousers and soft leather boots. She's wearing an oversized flannel shirt that's cinched around her waist with a braided leather belt that has a brass buckle. I love a girl who isn't afraid to dress like a tomboy when the occasion calls for it, and going to the docks to bring in fish calls for exactly the kind of getup Rachel chose to wear today.

"What have you got in there, a dead body?" she asks, as I enter the house and let my book bag drop to the floor with a thud. She bends to measure the weight of it and I am as lost as I always am at the sight of the mass of dark gypsy curls loosely gathered and falling halfway down her back. When she stands up, she looks at me with her huge brown eyes, and I swear I can see stars in them.

I slip off my coat and step out of my wet boots and put them side by side on the floor mat. The house is meagerly furnished. There's no coat rack in sight so I stuff my cap inside a jacket sleeve and place it neatly on top of my boots. *My mother would be proud.*

"Something smells great in here," I say, inhaling a waft of sizzling meat. I run my hands through my own shaggy hair, wishing I had thought to apply a little Brylcreem before I left the house.

"Mom's frying Spam," Rachel says. "Have you ever had it?"

I shake my head.

"It goes great with eggs. I hope you're hungry."

"Starving," I admit and follow her like a puppy into the kitchen.

Rachel's mom is at the stove and wearing a long white apron over her bathrobe. The apron is the same style as our butcher wears, only Mrs. Coulter's apron is minus blood stains.

"Good morning, Jonah," she calls over her shoulder, as she snaps a spoonful of Crisco into a hot skillet. Steam rises, fat hisses.

"Hello, Mrs. Coulter. Thanks for letting me come over this early."

She arranges four slices of the mystery meat into the pan, cracks open four eggs and adds them and promptly turns down the burner on the gas stove. Like all mothers, she can do a million things at once.

"I hope you haven't eaten breakfast yet," she says, pushing a long corkscrew curl away from her forehead with the back of her wrist. The first time I met Mrs. Coulter, I knew who Rachel had inherited her hair from.

"No, ma'am," I reply, hungrily eyeing the loaf of crusty bread I see her remove from the metal breadbox on the counter. She slices four generous slabs from the loaf and smears each one with sweet butter.

We hear the front door open, and seconds later we feel a draft swirl as a deep voice bellows from the foyer:—

"I'm back and as hungry as a bear!"

Professor Coulter's frame nearly fills the doorway to the kitchen; but for such a giant, the professor has one of the sunniest outlooks on life of anyone I know. When he smiles, his teeth show as large as piano keys, and his blue eyes become shaped like half moons. He has a folded copy of the daily paper tucked under his arm. He lays it on the counter to greet me.

"Well, hello there, Jonah!" he says, taking hold of my chapped hand and pumping it like the handle on an outdoor water pump. "I'm glad to see another man here to help us eat all this!"

In two strides he is at his wife's side, planting a hearty kiss on her mouth before turning to put an arm around Rachel, the apple of his eye.

"Hello, Kitten, how's my girl today? Would you pour your dad a cup of

72

coffee?" He asks before turning back to me. "How about you, Jonah—do you drink coffee or would you rather a Coke?"

"Coffee would be fine. Thank you, sir," I say, accepting the chair the professor has pulled out for me. He motions for me to sit down.

Mrs. Coulter places a hot platter of fried eggs and Spam in the center of the kitchen table and surrounds it with a basket of buttered bread, a bowl of apples, and four mugs of strong coffee. She removes her apron and takes her place at the table. Rachel's mom is a slightly older version of Rachel; both of them possess that dark gypsy hair that a guy (and bats) could get lost in.

I am careful not to help myself until the girls have taken what they want, and once again my mother's face comes to mind. We bow our heads while the professor recites a quick Jewish blessing, and then I pick up my fork to dig into this feast fit for a king. I spear a piece of Spam and pop it into my mouth.

"Careful, it's hot," Mrs. Coulter warns too late.

My tongue takes the burn, and I instantly suck in air, tumbling the scalding meat inside my mouth like a load of laundry. I take a swig of coffee, which only makes it worse, and feel the instant rise of a blister. My eyes water, but the flavor of the Spam is worth it. I eye the meat longingly and move the food around on my plate to help it cool.

"So what do you two have planned for *the grind?*" Professor Coulter asks, using teen lingo.

Rachel rolls her eyes and smiles. "By *grind*, I gather you mean our class science project?"

"I do." The professor breaks off a corner of bread and punctures the top of one perfect fried egg with it.

With my tongue still throbbing, I watch him sop up the runny egg yolk and plop the tasty morsel into his mouth.

"Jonah and I are going to submit a factual report with diagrams based on your theory that the eastern seaboard is at risk for a major storm, very possibly a *hurricane,* before the end of this year. Jonah has brought meteorology and astrology research books from the library."

"And how do you propose to prove it?" her father asks.

It's easy to see he and his wife are proud of their kid genius. Not only is Rachel smart, she's got a great pair of *gams*—even when they're being covered by a pair of pants.

"We're going to use the data you and mom compiled from your radio transmitters." She looks down and refers to some notes she scribbled on a pad. "We'll use what you submitted to the central Weather Bureau, in Washington, about the surface observations in the Caribbean, pointing out their direct connection to existing atmospheric conditions."

I am more confused than not, but I nod in agreement, as if I understand perfectly what was just said. I nurse the blister on my tongue, only too happy her parents didn't ask me to explain any of this.

"It sounds as though you've thought this through," Mrs. Coulter says, sipping her coffee. "However, be prepared to have your opinion met with a lot of skepticism. As we know, weather forecasting has yet to be developed, much less accepted by the public. We have a hard time convincing Washington that even though a hurricane or cyclone may appear as harmless, the chance of an epic storm of immense proportion is not only possible, but probable. The findings are serious and should not be taken lightly. Safety measures need to be taken now, should our predictions come true."

"What's the difference between them—hurricanes and cyclones?" I ask.

"They are one and the same, really, except for wind speed," Rachel answers, laying her fork beside her plate. "If the winds are more than seventy-four miles per hour, it's termed a *hurricane*. Traditionally, hurricanes form over the West Atlantic, bringing heavy winds and rains. *Cyclones* are circular movements of air that typically form over tropical water. And if you aren't confused enough, there are also *typhoons,* which are circular moving winds that typically form over the West Pacific."

"All hurricanes are cyclones, but not all cyclones are hurricanes," Professor Coulter comments. "However, it is the hurricane that delivers winds and rain at levels high enough to wreak incomprehensible havoc. They are capable of wiping out homes and flooding streets, of redefining the scope of nature, and of crippling economic production for indefinite amounts of time."

"Cape Cod has never witnessed a storm as bad as you're describing," I assure them. "We're pretty much known here for having fairly consistent weather. Even our nor'easters are manageable."

"Let's hope it will continue to be that way, but the odds are against it," Professor Coulter says. "We're not talking about nor'easters. The type of weather system Mrs. Coulter is describing is both potentially and phenomenally catastrophic. The type of massive fronts we're talking about call for specific conditions: warm, humid air movement, warm seas, and no obstructions of land in its way to slow it down." He reaches for an apple from the bowl on the table. Half of it is gone with the first bite.

All these scientific findings and premonitions about raging storms have me wondering about the Coulters and visionaries like them—genius minds sharing revolutionary beliefs in topics most people never even think about.

Whenever the Coulters talk weather, my brain becomes a sponge for science. I turn to Rachel. "Since we're writing a report on it, I suppose you know where the word *hurricane* came from."

"From the mythical god, Huracán, the god of evil," she answers, not skipping a beat. "He was a god feared above all others by Caribbean tribes." She makes a rough sketch of a toy top and pushes the pad to show me. "I thought we might use a top in our project to demonstrate how a hurricane's rotation works."

"I think we might still have one of those in the toy box in our attic," I tell her, "but how will we work it into our report?"

"A top has two movements, right? The rotation within, plus its forward motion, is what makes it work. It's the same with hurricanes. The wind inside the storm spirals around to create a tightly-spinning whirlwind. The closer the wind is to the center, the faster the hurricane or cyclone spins."

She looks at me to see if I understood and sees me grinning. *The babe is unbelievable!*

"Very good, Rachel," her father praises. "The wind outside the storm is an independent atmospheric force, pushing the disturbance forward in a specific direction and at a specific speed."

"In essence,' Mrs. Coulter adds, "the storm becomes a tropical cyclone— so devastating and so utterly powerful, it wipes out everything in its path. If it moves over the Atlantic, it becomes a hurricane. Wherever it touches down it has the potential to remap geography entirely."

"So, what do you think?" Rachel asks her parents, splaying her hands on the table as though confronting a jury. "Do you think we stand a chance at pulling an A?"

"No," her father says, shaking his head with conviction, "but definitely an A-plus."

Rachel locks two steely eyes on mine. "How about you, Jonah, what do you think?"

Me? I haven't felt this spooked since last week's episode of the Shadow. I say, "I think it's great; and thanks to your folks, we just might ace this project."

Grabbing two shiny apples from the bowl, I gently toss one to my girl. "Now, what do you say we grab the research books and find ourselves some big 'ol hurricanes?"

In truth, all I really want is to finally be alone with her.

Catherine

I return from working the food kitchen in town to find the kitchen table arranged with declarations of love. From Lizzie, a plate of cupcakes with pink runny frosting and two hastily-made Valentines fashioned from red construction paper and white paper doilies for her father and me; and from Jonah, a voucher to wash the car and do the dinner dishes for one month. It could have been a festive occasion had William been home tonight to share it.

As a result of one of our parishioners suffering a mishap when he lost his footing on a crumbling step outside the church, the council has called an immediate meeting to discuss repair options. The steps have been deteriorating for years and have reached the point where they have now become treacherous. Everyone knew it was only a matter of time until someone got hurt on them. None of the council, least of all William, cared that today is Valentine's Day or else they are all void of romance.

Some of us celebrate this trivial holiday of love, even if it is only with a decorated cupcake, a handmade Valentine or a promise to wash someone's dishes. What is important is that the people you love be remembered and, in turn, remember you.

A crocheted doll's dress, a new thermos, and a container of Union Leader pipe tobacco may not capture a heart, but they are gifts that, together with my attempt at making heart-shaped pancakes for breakfast, let my family know that I care enough to remember them on Valentine's Day. It has been a long day for me. My nerves are frayed, and so I am annoyed at having to spend the last few hours of it without my husband and some souvenir of his affections.

Unbeknownst to me, Lizzie ate two cupcakes and later took to her bed with a case of indigestion. Her mood was changeable today, with frequent bouts of emotion that required all of my coping skills. Lately she is fast to argue and even faster to weep. While it is not obvious, Lizzie's interest in boys is nevertheless underlying, and her complexion rebels with an occasional breakout. Eating two cupcakes will only exacerbate such episodes; however, it is every woman's prerogative to overdose on sugar from time to time.

Jonah, too, is taking full advantage of his father's absence. He has been holed up in the cramped half space of the coat closet in order to have privacy while talking on the telephone to Rachel Coulter. The only remnant of his presence in the house is the muffled fluctuation in his voice and the long black telephone cord lying in wait for an unsuspecting foot to trip over it.

Hopefully, for Jonah's sake, one of our nosey party line participants hasn't picked up her receiver and eavesdropped on the conversation with his girl. If they have, I will know it if they avoid making eye contact when we meet up in the market aisles.

If only I could have called on Frances tonight, but she is out this evening. Ellie Dickenson has a visiting cousin from Maine. Ellie is claiming to have scored 7600 on a game of Bridge, with a seven-level contract redoubled and down thirteen tricks while vulnerable. Frances, who has yet to take Ellie Dickenson at her word about anything, challenged her to a game of doubles. Frances never likes to lose.

Poor Frances! She has been white around the gills since I told her about Jack, though she says she understands how I could I have fallen prey to his charms. This is not to say that she made light of my impropriety. Clearly she disapproves, for she let me know how wounded she was that I had withheld from her this major impact on my life. When I told Frances the story from start to finish, she cried with me and we held on to each other like a pair of dotards. It just went to prove that when times get rough, we draw from the lifeline of staunch support we have always relied on receiving from one another. *Oh, of all the nights for William to be gone!*

Feeling void of affection and angry enough to pick a fight over it, my immediate remedy is a bubble bath to soothe my nerves.

William, who believes that a woman's drinking alone at home is a distasteful trait at best, is now the very reason I search for a bottle of red wine

78

from the limited selection he keeps stashed away in the cabinet in our dining room.

I select an inexpensive pinot noir. I am not as apt as William at uncorking a bottle, but I manage it without spilling any and give it a few minutes to breathe. I choose one of our best crystal wine glasses used only for company. Why not? Nothing should be too good for me tonight! I pour a goodly amount and head upstairs with the glass and the opened bottle of wine tucked under my arm.

As I pass the coat closet, I give a little rap on its door with my elbow. "Jonah, say goodnight to Rachel. You both have school tomorrow. You're holding up the party line."

He responds with an inaudible mumble I take for an assent, but I am too occupied with my own mission to ensure that he follow through. *Let his father deal with him when he gets home*, I think wearily, climbing the stairs and entering the bedroom where I savor a tasty sip of wine.

I set the glass and bottle on the dresser and cross the hall to the bathroom, where I sink the rubber stopper and turn the faucets on full force. Once the temperature has been adjusted to my liking, I reach for the chenille robe hanging behind the door and go back to my room to undress.

We have a full-length mirror behind our bedroom door. I strip and stand naked before it. The reflection that greets me there is kinder than I ever credit myself for. Maybe the wine has begun working its magic; I mind not at all what I see looking back at me.

I slip into the chenille robe and pull the belt tightly to cinch a waist that has remained fairly narrow, despite two pregnancies, and ceremoniously carry both wine glass and bottle to the bathroom. The feel of cold tile on my feet hastens my desire to get into the bath. I am as abundant with my use of hot water as with my ration of wine, both of which I would normally take care to conserve.

I scoop out a heaping capful of lavender salts and sprinkle it under the running water, followed by a capful of Castile liquid soap. Instantly the bubbles build, and a delicious fragrance permeates my surroundings. I lift a leg over the side of the tub to test the water, using my toes to gauge the temperature. The water feels as if it's been boiled in a cauldron. Perfect. Inch by inch I submerge myself, all the time thinking how easily troubles can be dispelled with a tub of hot water, a glass of wine, and the healing power of a simple garden scent.

As soon as I hear the reverberation of Jonah's heavy footsteps pass by the bathroom door and go into his room my entire body goes slack. The hypnotic drip, drip, dripping of the faucet has me closing my eyes. It is there, in the recesses of my mind, that I summon a Valentine of my own making—the *Rogue of Romance* himself, Jack Wakefield.

I am lying naked with Jack on his simple seaman's cot. We are alone on a boat, in the middle of nowhere, where we are free to explore each other's every want, every need.

Jack's body is over mine and I am melding to it with shameful wantonness. He is looking down on me with torment in his eyes—so deep, so raw, that I can but only study it for a moment before my face begins to burn with an admission of my own lust and I must turn my face away. His kisses are burning the skin of my neck as I lower my head to nibble the round of his shoulder. I can taste salt, and I bury my fingers deeply into the thick of his hair.

Slowly, Jack lets his head travel downward. He kisses the orbs of each breast, where he stops momentarily to tenderly tease each nipple before continuing down, down...

I can feel his damp tongue moving over the smooth plane of my stomach, the supple kisses of his sun-chapped lips leaving a fiery track upon my skin, already fevered with passion.

Grabbing feverishly at each other, our imaginary dialogue can be no more than a series of moans and mutterings, when...

...The sound of William's car pulling into the drive alerts me back to reality, my unfinished fantasy left to hover in the recess of my mind—only waiting on a moment's notice to continue.

I watch as the beams from the car's headlights pass like two ghosts across the airy bathroom curtain and hear the opening and closing of the car door. Seconds later, the front door opens and I make out the shuffling of a coat being hung on the coat rack.

Like a doe whose instinct tells her the hunter is near, I listen as William first walk into the parlor and then into the kitchen in search of me. He must have discovered the plate of cupcakes and the children's Valentine cards, for he remains there for several minutes until I finally hear the familiar footsteps coming up the stairs.

He pauses at the bathroom door and continues down the hall, first to check on Elizabeth, and then on to Jonah's room, where father and son converse in deep, low tones.

William raps his knuckle on the bathroom door to announce himself. When I don't answer, he opens the door just enough to allow his hand to pass through. With two fingers strategically positioned on its thorny stem, he passes a long red rose through the narrow passage.

"Are you decent?" he asks.

Silence.

Warily, William's well-groomed head peeks around the corner. His bashful expression irritates me enough that I sink even lower beneath the suds until only my head and the glass of wine I am holding are visible in my tomb of iridescent froth.

He enters the room and shuts the door behind him. He observes the open bottle of wine near the base of the tub, but he knows better than to ask what it's doing there.

"I'm sorry, the meeting ran longer than expected," is all the explanation he offers before reaching over to present me with the rose.

"Let me guess," I say, taking the proffered stalk and tipping its partially open bud to my nose, "you stole this from the church?"

"I did," he replies sheepishly, "but I had the sense to wait until all the others had left. No one saw me take it."

I sniff the irresistible blossom while maneuvering the toes of one wrinkled foot under water and using them like fingers to pull the chain on the stopper. Instantly the drain makes a deep sucking noise as the tub begins slowly to empty out, swallowing the last of my reverie.

"However," William says, reaching into the pocket of his cardigan and pulling out a small black box with a red bow on top, "this is paid for, fair and square." He holds up the gift for me to see.

"Please hand me that towel behind you," I ask, ignoring him.

William reaches behind him for the towel, and I lean over the tub to place my wine glass carefully on the floor. He offers his hand to me, which I also ignore. Applying concentrated effort, I lift myself as gracefully as I can up and out of the tub. Patches of tiny sparkling suds stick to my limbs and my torso, which appear flushed and rosy pink. Transfixed, William clears his throat.

Tucking the jewelry box under his chin, he holds open the fluffy towel. Demurely, I step into it, taking the two corners from his hands and crossing each end to secure them under my arms. My hair, which I had loosely pinned up with a barrette, had come undone while bathing. I raise a hand to wipe away a few damp tendrils that are clinging to my nape.

William hands me the small package and moves behind me. Holding me tightly against him, he rests his chin on my shoulder to watch while I deftly remove the bow and purposely sigh as if the token is of little consequence. Both of us know, however, that I am more than a little intrigued.

It is a Bulova wristwatch with a stretch band to replace the relic I owned until two weeks ago when it finally stopped running for the last time. I am touched to think he even remembered that my old watch had broken. I turn forgivingly to face him.

"This is lovely, William. Thank you." I slip on the brand new watch, turning my wrist from side to side, noting how its newness gleams beneath the soft glow of the bathroom light.

"Now you can keep an accurate account of my comings and goings." I feel him slide a cool hand under the towel and boldly run it up my thigh.

"As if I needed any watch for that," I say, swatting away his impertinence.

"I am late, it's true, but you've been drinking," he says, brushing aside the damp hairs on my neck with his lips. "I should think we are equally guilty parties."

"And who drove me to it?" I ask huskily, turning slightly to allow him better access to the smooth curvature of my throat.

Against my thigh, I can feel William's ardor growing stronger. My own intoxication is such that for a moment I forget who is kissing me—-Jack or William, just as I am unsure as to which I am experiencing—fantasy or reality?

"Come to bed," William moans, releasing the towel and allowing it to drop in a heap at my feet, "and be my valentine."

It is not often enough my husband is this creative or this tender in his foreplay. I shiver, sliding my arms into the robe he holds open for me. Reluctantly I allow myself to be led to our bed, where I surrender myself to William and to the night.

Fleetingly, and without my even missing it, my shipboard fantasy with Jack Wakefield quickly fades into the void of nothingness from whence it came.

Frances

With spare time she did not have, Catherine came over as soon as I telephoned her. I pour her a cup of tea at my kitchen table while she peruses the letter I have just received from Edward.

"I am not sure I understand exactly what he is asking for," she says, "but his letter seems cordial enough."

"He is hinting, as he always does. Don't you see? He wants me to secure his inheritance, only this time he is suggesting he come with me to see my attorney!"

Even a short explanation has my stomach in turmoil, and I hobble to the cabinet in search of my bicarbonate of soda.

"Do you see the part where he mentions the Parisian boarding school? The child is not even born yet, and already they've got its bags packed up and enrolled in a private school! Paris, no less! I say that's Blanche talking, I'm sure of it!"

Fuming, I mix a heaping spoonful of bicarbonate into a glass of water, nearly cracking the glass with the spoon as I stir it. I watch it fizz until it's dissolved, then I gulp half of it down and burp.

"Be a dear and take this glass to the table for me, would you, Catherine?" Immediately she is at my side, taking the glass from my hand.

"In defense of Edward and Blanche, do you really blame either for counting on their good fortune when they have a wealthy and, I say this lovingly, a somewhat aging relation?"

"I may be Edward's only living relative, and a wealthy one at that, but Edward is not the only person I could consider leaving my fortune to." I slap my hand on the table. "Oh! And did you read the part where he says he must take Blanche away for a few weeks to get some sun? He plans to take her on a cruise, aboard the Queen Mary, as soon as the baby can be left with a nurse! Do they know how costly an excursion like that will be? I assure you, this is not one of Edward's highfaluting ideas. It is no wonder he is looking for a monetary lifeline, but he is foolish to count on his benefactress being *me!*"

"Now you're just talking nonsense," Catherine says. "Edward is blood; he's family."

"That doesn't make him entitled," I point out. "I'd like to know what he and Blanche would have to say if, for instance, I were to leave the bulk of my estate to you."

I can tell I have embarrassed her, for the cat's got Catherine's tongue. A look of confusion passes like a summer breeze over her face, but then she throws back her head and lets out a bawdy laugh.

"Me? What would I do if I had your money? Why, I can't possibly begin to fathom it!"

"Indulge me, just for fun," I ask her.

Catherine sobers, bringing her elbows up on the table so she can cradle her chin in her hands. She looks up at the ceiling, pondering my question for a moment before looking back at me.

"I come from simple stock, Frances. I'm afraid that is all I have ever known."

"Oh, come on. Surely you can do better than that," I say, feeling feisty with the remedial results of the bicarbonate. "Tell me. What doors could be opened to you if you had a sizeable income that was entirely yours? Would you use it to travel? Maybe see the world? What flights of fancy could you make come true with that kind of money?" When she doesn't answer, I help her imagination. "Why, you could renovate your entire home. How about a closet, specifically built to your needs, that you could fill with the all the latest fashions—dresses, shoes, and furs. Think about it."

"I doubt that would do much for me. I believe one doesn't miss what one never had." She reaches over to take hold of my hand and massages my fingers absentmindedly. "As long as my children are healthy, and I have the love of a good man, what more could I need?"

"To which man do you refer?"

"Always the fox, aren't you? That is why you are my best friend, Frances. No one knows me as you do. In answer to your question, I can honestly say I would spend your inheritance wherever it would do the most good. Who knows what will be coming down the road with this crazy Hitler? Already he is at odds with Europe. What if our country chooses to become involved? Fathers, husbands, brothers and sons may all be called upon to serve. How ethical is it, I suppose, to help one well-to-do relative when there are so many who have so much less and are in need?"

"And *that*, Catherine dear, is why you are my best friend. You understand the big picture. Unlike Blanche and Edward, both of whom are self-centered, you are sensible and caring. You think about the welfare of others before you consider your own."

We sit in silence for a moment, secure in each other's company. Finally I say:—

"I know Edward worries about how the potential for war will affect his job. As a boy he saw what havoc the Great Depression wreaked on his father and the banking industry. If Edward has invested wisely and his job is secure, then any children he and Blanche produce will be provided for. He should not be searching for a golden egg nor count on me to play the part of the hen."

"I'm sorry, Frances, but I should get going," Catherine says, rising from her chair. "Is there anything I can get for you before I leave?"

Such a short visit is unusual for us. I think perhaps this topic has made my friend uncomfortable.

"Oh! Must you? I was going to serve some of the luscious strudel Mary baked yesterday. I was hoping you would stay to have a slice with me. Is everything all right at home?"

"It's fine; I need to find Jonah is all. Cynthia Brighton needs him to clean out her potting shed this afternoon. I've got to drive to the dock to pick him up and deliver him at her place. Not to mention William must be pulling his hair out by now. Lizzie is acting very cantankerous these days."

I detect a slight quiver in her lip and know there is something more she is not telling me.

"Is there something you want to talk about?" I query.

"No. Thank you, though." She hands me Edward's letter. "I know you will make the right decision about this. Just pray on it."

She bends to kiss my forehead, and I close my eyes to receive Catherine's blessing. Her lips, as pliable and soft as a child's, feel cool on my own troubled brow.

I remain seated like this, my eyes closed, until I hear her close the front door behind her. Catherine's signature scent, Lavender, remains.

"I wish you could have stayed on, dearest friend," I whisper," warm tears filling my eyes and leaving me to think how both of us are in our own secret hell.

Only when the kitchen is bathed in the deep purple hues of evening do I finally rise up from my chair, the pain in both hips letting me know I have been sitting here far too long.

I apply my crutches and walk myself to the counter to flip on the light switch. There I catch my reflection in the glass of the kitchen window. A long, drawn expression looks back at me. As pathetic a notion as it is, my image likeness makes me feel less lonely. I smile and it smiles back, adding to the illusion that there is someone else in the house with me and that I am not, after all, utterly alone.

Jonah

Rachel and I are standing on the dock when I recognize our family car approaching faster than either of my parents drive. As it nears, I can see my mother's stern expression behind the wheel. She is honking the horn to get my attention, even though I waved to her. As she pulls up to the dock, Rachel and I hang over the railing and look down into the open window of the car where Mother beckons with her finger.

She has the passenger door has already opened for us as we descend the steps. She acknowledges Rachel with little more than a nod and says to me:—

"Get in; I'm taking Rachel home."

"But we just got here," I say. "The fishing boats will be coming in any minute."

"Mrs. Brighton has some work that needs doing. You and Rachel can see each other some other time."

"Can I at least drive?"

"You may not. I will drive Rachel home. Get in."

We pull up in front of the Coulters' house. Mother leaves the car running and taps her fingernails on the steering wheel. *This isn't good,* I think to myself as I help Rachel step out of the car and escort her to her front door.

On our way up the sidewalk Rachel says, "Something's wrong. Your Mother's angry. What have you done?"

"I have no idea. Maybe Lizzie's acting up and it put her knickers in a twist, I don't know."

When I'm back in the car and we're on the road, I sneak a peek at my mother from out of the corner of my eye. She looks as though she could fry an egg on her head. I know something is really wrong when we bypass the turn to the Brighton's house and take the first deserted road we come to. Mother shuts off the car motor and turns to face me. Her expression is stiff, and her lips couldn't be tighter if she glued them together. She stares at me.

"What's the matter?"

She bends over, reaches under the driver's seat, and comes up holding a brown paper bag.

"Open it," she orders, handing me the bag with two fingers as though it contains a dead animal.

I take the bag from her and feel its light weight, trying to gauge its contents. I'm at a loss, my mind racing to think what could be inside. Carefully I unravel the wrinkled rolled top and peer in.

Money! At first glance, it doesn't make sense. And then I realize what it is. It's the two hundred-fifty dollars I had stashed in a pair of socks in my dresser. *How the hell did she find it?*

"Mother, I—"

"Where did you get this, Jonah? And don't you dare even think about lying to me!"

"I've been saving up—-"

"Liar!" she screams, and I feel the sting of the hand I never saw coming. I press my palm to my cheek while I look at her through a film of tears.

"You stole this from church, didn't you?"

No sense in lying—she knows.

"Yes," I confess.

"How could you?" Mother shrieks. "Whatever in the world possessed you to do such a thing?" She slaps my arm with her closed fist so hard it feels more like a punch. "You know better than to steal—and from a *church!* If your father knew, he would be as mortified as I am!" She drops her head in her hands, and stifled sob escapes her.

"Mother, I—I'm so sorry!" I try to explain, but she holds up a hand to stop my apology mid-sentence.

My eyes try to convey the words she won't allow me to speak. Again she drops her head to her chest and cries. She has every right to be ashamed of me, and my heart breaks to see her so hurt—worse, to know that I'm the cause of it. There is nothing I can say in my defense. We stay like this for some time, neither of us talking or looking at each other, both of us ashamed of the same person.

When my mother finally raises her head, her eyes appear unseeing, like the kid who once lived in our town who was hit hard with a flying baseball and always stared into space after that. She runs her fingers under her eyes and dabs her nose on her wrist before reaching into her pocket to bring out a folded white envelope. When she's composed, she hands the envelope to me and leans her face close to mine. She says:—

"Put the money in here and seal the envelope. I am going to drive you to the church, where you are going slip this envelope through the slot in the office door. When your father goes there tomorrow and finds it, he will think there has been an anonymous donation from some generous soul."

My stomach knots as I wait for the other shoe to fall. There must be more punishment coming, since I can't remember ever having seen my mother this angry.

"You are to tell your father you no longer want to pass the basket at church—say you would rather spend the time praying about your vocation; he will believe that. Then, you spend that time each week on your knees, asking God to forgive you. I only hope He can!"

She closes her eyes to steady her breathing, and when she speaks again her, it is in a lower tone. "You have been raised better than this."

Almost instantly, her anger resurfaces. Reaching over, she twists my jacket sleeve fast and so tightly in her fist, she catches the skin of my arm. I feel the pinch and wince in pain.

"You will never, ever, *ever* steal another thing again! Is that understood? Do you hear me? If you so much as even *think* about doing something like this again, Jonah, I swear I will turn you in to the police myself, so help me God!"

When we leave the church and head for the Brighton's house, my cheek is still smarting from my mother's slap, and I know without seeing it that the top of my arm is sporting a black and blue mark the size of a nickel. She says I am to come home as soon as I have finished whatever chores need doing, then drives off without so much as a goodbye.

I walk up to the Brighton's front door and knock. When it opens, I'm surprised to see Alice Brighton standing there rather than her mother. Alice looks like a pinup girl. She's dressed in a cherry red jumpsuit and a pair of stacked high heels. I'm eye level with her cleavage, and it's hard to look away from that. I force myself to look up and immediately I can see that she has noticed the imprint of my mother's hand on my cheek. Thankfully she doesn't mention it, but she's smiling that wicked smile of hers.

"You should see the other guy," I joke.

Alice says nothing. She simply looks at me with those huge Betty Boop eyes of hers as if I am Spencer Tracy or Clark Gable and she's Katharine Hepburn.

We hear Mrs. Brighton's voice from somewhere inside the house. "Is that Jonah?"

"Hello, Mrs. Brighton!" I call back, shifting my weight from one foot to the other. Alice has yet to speak a single word.

"Alice, dear," her mother calls out, "show Jonah what I want done in the shed, will you? I'm sorry I can't come out there myself, Jonah, but I have just washed my hair!"

Alice is still just standing there, looking like a lollipop good enough to eat.

"So? Are you going to show me, or what?" I ask, looking up at her with my thumbs hooked in my back pockets.

"Yeah, sure," she says, smooth as silk. "Follow me."

If her voice was a food, it would be melted chocolate. She steps out onto the stoop, moving like she's walking on stilts, and I think her legs must be long enough to reach heaven.

"You might want to put on a coat," I tell her. "It's colder than a witch's tit out here."

"I'm hot enough," she says, purposely brushing up against me as she leads the way across the lawn toward the shed. The rolling motion of her hips reminds me of the buoys on the bay during high tide.

The shed is small, dank, and dimly lit. It consists of four walls and a tin roof built on an earthen floor as hard as rock. There are two elevated beds rustically built with a few faded boards and some nails. Each bed is filled with hardened soil; when it's turned, it's for starting seedlings.

There's a potting bench overflowing with hand tools, a rickety table loaded with bags of mulch and potting soil, and at least fifty clay pots in assorted sizes stacked or thrown around the place. Besides all this there are rakes, shovels, and a wheelbarrow with an old metal watering can hanging from one of its handles. Cobwebs hang from every corner, especially across the dirty windows, and a spattering of mouse droppings can be found on just about every available surface.

It smells like a tomb in here, and I can't see a single living organism in sight, least of all anything that grows——maybe with the exception of mold. Still, the old shed holds a certain appeal for me in a primitive, caveman sort of way.

Alice, who hasn't taken her eyes off me since I arrived, sashays closer. Her perfume is overpowering, yet intoxicating. She asks in a husky voice:——

"So, what do you say? You want the job, or what?"

"I dunno know...maybe. I guess it depends on what needs to be done in here."

She waves a pointed finger through the air like a wand, affording me an even stronger whiff of her cheap perfume.

"It looks like a pigsty. I'm fairly sure my mother wants you to clean it out. You know, stack the pots, weed the beds and rake them out, sweep away the cobwebs, and kill the spiders."

"Kill the spiders? But they're important," I say, watching her eyes grow wide. "They feed on the bugs that eat plants. You're not afraid of an itsy bitsy spider, are you?" We're standing so close that I can see the light sprinkling of freckles across the bridge of her nose. I want badly to reach out and touch her.

"I'm afraid of anything that bites," she whispers, tickling my ear lobe with her lips and leaning into me.

"I don't bite," I croak. I can feel myself growing hard.

"I didn't think so," she says, wrapping her arms around my neck and moving in for a kiss.

I know I should resist her coming on to me, but I can't. The feel of her velvety tongue in my mouth has me so turned on that I'm unaware that she is unbuckling my belt and unzipping my pants until they are down around my knees.

Backing me into the wood of the wobbly old table, Alice slides down the front of me, like water off a duck's back, and takes me in her mouth. The shock stops my heart cold, so delicious is the sensation. Feeling dizzy, I lean backward for support, sending a tall stack of heavy clay pots crashing to the ground. Seconds later we hear Mrs. Brighton's voice shouting out the kitchen window.

"What happened? Is everything all right out there?"

Alice bolts upright, pressing a finger to my lips. "Yes, Mama," she yells back, "everything's fine!"

We stand there, as still as statues, listening for approaching footsteps. When they don't come, Alice turns back to me, look at me with questioning eyes. Should she continue?

When I don't answer, Alice's expression changes to that of a sly fox; and in one fluid motion, she slithers back down on her knees.

Frances

Bentley used to look for reasons to stop at the law firm of Walker, Coffer & Reid in order to spend time in the firm's judicial conference room. Three partners had purchased the seventeenth century house and invested a tidy sum to replicate the structure of an old English design. Though I had never been inside the building, Bentley assured me it rivaled any prestigious law firm he had seen during his years in finance.

Of course, it was Bentley who always took care of our business dealings and any strings that were subsequently attached. I never minded relinquishing my funds into his hands, for it was in his best interest to keep a careful watch over our equity if he wished to perpetuate a cash flow that knew no bounds.

After Bentley's untimely death, the firm's head attorney, Philip Walker, Esq., accommodated me in my unexpected widowhood by bringing me any legal documents requiring my signature.

Today, however, our business together is a horse of a different color. It is official business that cannot wait until Philip finds time to come to me. Thanks to my housekeeper's kind escort, I am here now and do not have to wait days to be given Philip's wise counsel.

With the impertinent letter from Edward in my purse, I allow a seemingly rigid secretary of the firm to usher me into the conference room I have heard so much about. She is an austere woman, who seats me at the table and offers me coffee, which I gratefully accept, though my animation extracts no smile from her dour face. I glance admiringly as she exits the room on stilted heels, her gliding, free-flowing walk the cause of my instant envy. Softly, she closes the door behind her, and I take time to look around the room my husband always so admired.

The dark mahogany walls and ornate moldings are reminiscent of Old English architecture. It is a masculine decor for the legal minds of those who have spent endless billable hours in this room. Two walls boast bookshelves that house volumes of leather-bound law books with uniform bindings of navy and red leather titled in gold leaf. I find myself wondering who has the harder time of it—the lawyers who must reference these hundreds of books or the secretary assigned to keeping them dusted?

Portraits of the firm's founding partners, forever captured in oils, hang on the walls in heavy gilded frames. The artist's rendition has each somber-looking magistrate looking directly into the eyes of both counselor and client, the judicial expression in their own eyes never leaving those of the beholder.

The main focus in this historic room, however, is the long cherry conference table. Its highly-polished surface is as hard and glossy as a pond frozen over; twelve handsomely matched leather chairs encircle it, one of which I am comfortably occupying.

There is a gentle knock on the door and a receptionist in the bloom of youth enters with a small coffee tray. She places it carefully on the table and leaves the room just as Philip Walker enters with his easy stride. Philip's charm is still evident at sixty-five years old; he has barely aged in all the time I've known him. Philip's favored companion, a perfectly groomed Irish setter named Dublin, trots closely and silently at his owner's heels, as Philip takes my hand and bends to kiss my cheek.

"Frances, you are looking exceptionally well," he tells me.

"As are you, dear friend," I reply, in kind. "I hope you can forgive me for dropping by without calling for an appointment."

"You know you are always welcome, though I would have come to you had you only asked. Your business must be urgent to bring you here."

I assure him it is and ask after his family. Dublin has been wagging his tail, sniffing quizzically at my crutches before trying to lift my hand with his snout in an obvious ploy to get me to pet him. Philip orders the dog to go with a snap of his fingers, but I am quick to pull a small morsel of wrapped biscuit from my purse. I expose the treat, and Dublin gazes pleadingly at his master, who nods his permission. Ever so gently, the dog accepts the treat from me, taking it between his big teeth and then disappearing under the table to form a furry circle of warmth at my feet.

I pull Edward's letter from my purse and hand it to my attorney. "I would like you to assess this before I tell you the reason why I am here."

It is both comical and somewhat disturbing to watch Philip Walker, senior partner and former Rhodes Scholar, looking for a loophole in a letter he no doubt finds inconsequential. He studies it as though he has been asked to translate Egyptian hieroglyphics, but I know his trained eye is looking for any part of the note that might be incriminating. His intuitiveness puts my troubled mind at ease, for I know Philip understands full well it is not the significance of the letter that could potentially be problematic, but the high stakes that would be won if I were to sign off on its demands.

I know enough to keep silent while Philip shuffles through a manila folder he's brought with him, marked *Gellermont.* I watch him spread the various legal forms and typewritten pages upon the gleaming table top. Quickly, he peruses Edward's letter once more, simultaneously scribbling notes on a legal pad with the fountain pen Bentley and I brought him one year when we were in France. Finally, Phillip raises his eyes and peers at me over wire-rimmed spectacles, the furrow in his forehead lifting like a question mark.

"Apart from taking somewhat of a brazen stand, it seems Edward is asking for nothing more than he believes is already coming to him, really, though he may be trying to ensure his position by using a cunning bit of leverage; namely, the child he and his wife are expecting."

"Read between the lines, my friend," I insist, stomping the tip of one of my crutches on the oriental carpet. The rug is so thick that my exclamation of annoyance is delivered in silence. "Clearly it is not Edward talking, though he has penned the words himself. It is that greedy wife of his, Blanche, and her highbrow ways. She is a self-centered spendthrift, hell-bent on securing my estate to use for her own extravagances!"

"All I am saying is that——"

"My only living relative is the likely choice to inherit?" I finish his sentence for him, my eyes dark with anger. "Edward may be the apparent heir, but he is not my only choice; and that, kind sir, is exactly what I have come here today to discuss."

"Your estate is yours to bestow as you see fit, Frances, though I would advise you not to decide anything when your emotions are running high." As though to calm me, Philip takes a moment to remove his spectacles and massage his eyes. It is apparent the years have left their mark. "Are you proposing a codicil?" he asks.

"I daresay I am talking more than a *codicil,*" I say, correcting my posture in the chair. "I am here to revise my entire Last Will and Testament!"

Philip pales. "You cannot be serious."

"Oh, but I most certainly am," I say.

"You wish to revise your entire Will because of this one letter from Edward?"

"No, not because of the letter, Philip; I wish to revise my Will so that I can die knowing my money is where it can do the most good. The changes I wish to make should meet with your approval when you hear what they are. If you do not agree after I have finished explaining them, I will of course take your opposition into consideration."

"But what of Edward's proposal?" he asks, extending the letter toward me. "Are you planning to respond to this?"

"I'm not, but you should," I say, waving his hand away. "I refuse to be dictated to by the likes of my nephew. Edward will just have to wait until I die to know how this story ends." I say, petting Dublin, who has reappeared at my side in search of another treat. "In the meantime, I shall derive immense pleasure from knowing that Blanche will be chomping at the bit just waiting for me to kick the bucket!"

Catherine

Finding time to take for myself is a luxury these days. When I pass it by, the hallway mirror reflects the strain I've been under. Obviously it is going take all of the next few months to improve my appearance in time for Jack's visit. Call me what you will, but I do wish to look just right for him.

To see me now, he would think what a dregs I've become, I think, smoothing my hands over my small, but sagging, breasts. Nothing will do but that Jack Wakefield should be heartbroken when he sees the beauty he once loved and never should have left behind.

The smell of wet animal permeates the room. Without warning, Jonah's form appears in the mirror behind my shoulder. He is as filthy as a street urchin, and I can only be grateful that at least he remembered to leave his dirty boots at the door.

"You're home," I say, mildly annoyed at having been caught preening.

There is something different about him. Is it pride? I should think the thrashing I gave him in the car this afternoon would have taken the wind out of his sails. But here he stands, looking fairly pleased with himself.

He places two bills and two quarters on the table and gives me a single nod of his head.

"I trust that is your pay?"

"Two dollars and fifty cents," he answers proudly. "It figures out to be exactly one percent of what I stole from church. It's for you."

"You've already paid your debt to the church, remember? This is money you earned," I say, sliding the currency off the table and handing it back to him. "You have earned it honestly; it's yours to keep."

Jonah takes the money and pockets it.

"Now, please go bathe—and wash your hair," I remind him. "You smell like something the cat dragged in."

"We don't have a cat," he says.

"Off with you now," I say, waving him away one finger. "Come back when you look decent and I'll give you something to eat. You must be hungry."

"Starving," he says on his way out of the room.

"I'll have a snack ready. Nothing too heavy; we're having roast pork for dinner."

Once again, my back is to him when Jonah enters the kitchen within the hour. As before, I can smell him before I see him, but this time it is the fresh, wholesome scent of skin scrubbed clean with bar soap and plenty of hot water.

I turn around, expecting to experience a nostalgic remnant of Jonah when he was a boy—fresh out of the tub, with rosy cheeks and towel-dried hair that stands all on end. But there is no little boy in this room, only a young man, and I shudder as if a ghost has just walked over a grave. I look at my son, with his wet hair slicked back, and I am looking at Jack Wakefield, just as he looked when we were growing up.

"Are you all right?" Jonah asks. "You seem off."

"I'm fine," I answer, handing him the peanut butter and jelly sandwich I prepared for him.

"Thanks—I'm really famished," he says, eliminating a quarter of the sandwich in one bite.

"Dinner won't be long," I announce.

Jonah helps himself to a Coke from the ice box and easily pops its cap with his thumb. "Where's Lizzie?"

"Your Father has taken her to her dance class. She has been after him for months now to watch her perform."

"That's good; Father should do more of that sort of thing," Jonah says, coming to stand beside me.

He takes a swig from the bottle and finishes the last of the sandwich while leaning against the counter to watch me peel potatoes. I can tell he has something on his mind, so I leave the quiet moment between us while I wipe the peels from the sink and dump them in the garbage. Finally, I break the silence.

"So? Do you have anything to say for yourself? I should think you would."

"What would you like to hear, besides how sorry I am?" he asks earnestly.

I rinse the peeled potatoes and roll them in a towel to dry. "Explaining what possessed you to steal might be a good place to start."

"Honestly? I don't know." He puts his empty plate in the sink, shoves his hands deep in his pockets and looks down at his feet. "I've been pillaging from the collection for a while," he admits. "Not every Sunday, but often enough."

I stop what I am doing and look at him, my mouth agape. His confession has me believing I must be looking at a total stranger.

"Jonah, I can't believe this, not of *you!* Surely you knew what you were doing was wrong—very, very wrong!"

"Of course I did," my son admits. "It was something that got easier to do once I saw how easy it was. I know that's no excuse."

I take a breath and exhale, wondering how any child of mine, with a minister father, could do something so blatantly dishonest. And suddenly I realize that the question is not *how* he did it, but *why?* As parents, how much of it is our own doing? *Where had William and I failed our son?*

"Was it your way of lashing out after our telling you about...Jack?"

He covers his face with his hands and he drags them downward in an expression of fatigue. "I admit, sometimes I wish you never had told me. But I'm also glad you did. I know you had to—that you thought it was time I knew the truth." He lowers his eyes again to avoid looking at me.

"How do you feel about it now that you know?" I ask, unsure that I am ready for his reply.

"I don't know. I'm not sure—confused, I guess."

The smell of roasting meat tells me it time to add the potatoes. Jonah's remark is left hanging in the air while I open the oven door and remove the roast. I place the pan on top of the stove. The roast sizzles loudly, its crusty skin spraying a halo of hot grease around itself in a fine mist. I cut the potatoes and place them around the meat, rolling each half in the savory drippings that have begun to pool around its sides.

"Will you tell me about him?" Jonah asks.

"What is it exactly that you would you like to know?" I ask, hoping his interest is general and that I will not falter with my answer.

He thinks for a moment. "What was he like? What was it about Jack that attracted you to him?"

I lift my apron to dry my hands and motion for my son to sit with me at the kitchen table. He is looking to me to answer while I am scrambling for the right words to describe a man he has never met. How could I even begin to explain what I myself don't understand? Gathering my thoughts quickly, I make this analogy:—

"When I was eleven, my father took me to Atlantic City to see the Ringling Brothers Circus. I was fascinated to be there. The sights! The sounds! The costumes! I'll never forget the smell inside that monstrous tent and what it felt like to be holed up inside. It reeked of wild animals, of sweat, and beer, mixed with the tantalizing aroma of popcorn, candy apples, and cotton candy. Three different acts were performed in three rings and all at the same time. As one finished, another would come out from behind the curtain to take their place in the ring. Necks were straining not to miss a single stunt that was being announced by the shrill whistle blown by the ring leader—a strikingly handsome man with a mustache—garbed in white tights and high black boots, a bright red jacket with a white cravat and a tall black hat. Whips snapped, and tigers jumped through hoops of fire. Commands were shouted, and elephants rose up on their two back legs, trumpeting ear-splitting salutes with their trunks. Beautiful ladies rode white Arabian stallions with jewel-studded reins and colorful clowns made fun of each other and heckled the crowds. But the best was the great trapeze act, led by my father's childhood friend. It was a trio of acrobats: two men and one woman, who flew through the air with the greatest of ease from forty feet off the ground! Each of them would swoop down off the pedestal on their bar to somersault through the air to clasp the opposite trapeze in the nick of time. Every stunt was performed with exact precision. It was absolutely thrilling!"

"I would give my eye teeth to see something like that!" Jonah exclaims, wide-eyed. "Do you think Father would take us if the circus ever comes to Cape Cod?"

"The circus is so big, it would have come to Boston, but I sincerely doubt your father wouldn't want to see it," I confess. "Your father believes circus performers to be a shady lot: lost souls, walking around half-naked, trying to corrupt a dignified society. Somehow I cannot envision him sitting in the audience enjoying himself."

"That's too bad," Jonah replies. "Father could use a little letting loose. He is so serious—about everything. Grandfather was a sport, though, wasn't he?"

"That he was. He would have adored you and your sister, too, but let me tell you the rest of my story. At the end of the show, when the tent was emptied of the crowds, we descended the bleachers, and my father led me around two of the massive rings, now strewn with straw and animal droppings, to the third ring where the aerial equipment was set up. I was introduced to his friend, Mr. Botillini, a small, wiry man dressed in bright blue tights and a sequined shirt. For a few moments he and my father spoke quietly over my head. Then, with a signal from Mr. Botillini, one of the acrobats up above lowered two trapeze bars from the ceiling until they hung just twenty feet above the safety net, while another lowered the pedestals and ladders on either side to a safe level. Your grandfather, squatting to his knees until his face was level with mine, asked me if I would like to fly."

"I can't believe you never told me this story!" Jonah exclaimed, his eyes growing wider still. "Weren't you terrified?"

"Not me! The female acrobat took me behind a curtain and helped me change into one of her trainers outfits. Mr. Botillini gave me careful instruction, none of which I can now recall. I remember the words *prêt* and *hup* being shouted each time I was passed from one acrobat to the other. They took turns grabbing hold of either my hands or my feet and never missed a beat of timing. Even if one of them had made a mistake, I knew there was a huge safety net below, so that when one of them said they were letting go, I simply fell into that great net and bounced harmlessly."

"That is amazing! Imagine, flying through the air! I can't wait to tell Rachel about this!"

I feel my face immediately cloud over. "Jonah, you never repeated to Rachel what we told you about your...parentage, did you?"

"You told me not to, so I didn't," he says. But I am not sure I believe him and wonder if he can now add *liar* to his list of shortcomings.

"I don't understand what the trapeze story has to do with the man who fathered me," Jonah says, clearly trying to make a connection.

"It's just that being airborne on that trapeze was the most exhilarating experience of my life. At least it was until that first summer when my father brought me to Cape Cod. There I met a handsome young man, who looked exactly like *you*. His name was Jack Wakefield, and he was more exciting than any adventure I had ever known."

Jonah

The retelling of my mother's adventure on a flying trapeze has given me a renewed outlook on life—that, plus a half-toss with Alice Brighton in the potting shed. Don't get me wrong, it's not that I am proud of myself for allowing Alice to do what she did; but show me a guy who would turn down the advances of a willing babe, and I'll show you a guy with a screw loose. Besides, it's not like Rachel was going to make whoopee with me anytime soon. I can barely get to first base with her, and we've been courting for months. She keeps telling me she's got a set of values, which translated means: *hands off, buster*. Truthfully, I respect her for it; I really do.

It was great to wake up today to Mother Nature supplying the ideal weather conditions for Rachel and me to deliver our science project summation to the class. It's raining cats and dogs, and there is just enough wind out there to add a touch of suspense. The curtain of rain is like the perfect backdrop for our speech on hurricanes. Thanks to Rachel and her parents, we're bound to earn the A+ we're hoping for, unless our science teacher, Mr. Kellington, finds our topic choice a bit farfetched. I certainly think our project beats any others I can see coming through the door as I wait for Rachel in the school lobby.

Nancy Mildauer and Billy Curran come in carrying a fishbowl with two goldfish in it. They say they plan to demonstrate the retention of learned behavior in fish. What supplies were needed for that: a fish bowl, a couple of goldfish and some water? And yet I notice the goldfish already seem to be making a *big splash* (get it?) with the students. It's a lot less work to put two fish in a bowl than what Rachel and I had to do to prepare.

The class clown, Dick Gillespie, is paired off with Marge Roemer, the shyest girl in our entire school. They came through the door balancing a wooden box between them, in which they have planted assorted seeds. They told me the purpose is to show how quickly the seeds sprout under various temperatures and in different liquids. Most of the seedlings I saw were already floating, and Dick and Marge arrived looking like two drowned rats.

There are laboratory demonstrations—interesting rocks and fossils—and some projects involving chemicals. But the one I predict will give Rachel and me a run for our money is the one on Egyptian mummification. It's being presented by two of the smartest kids in class, John McCarthy and Barbara Duggan. They took a doll, wrapped it in tea stained gauze bandages, and made a hand-painted mummy box to lay it in. They have drawings of the torturous-looking instruments used by the Egyptians to remove vital organs from the dead bodies by way of the nose, mouth and stomach, and they brought pieces of leather, which they had covered with a mixture of sand and salt to demonstrate how the Egyptians thought to preserve flesh before sealing their relatives away for eternity. What a cool project! How do some people come up with these ideas?

"Hey," I hear coming from a small voice behind me, accompanied by a tap on my shoulder as gentle as an acorn falling from a tree.

I turn to find Rachel standing there, dripping wet, wearing a raincoat that appears to be two sizes too large for her. Under her arm is a wet brown paper bag with the colorful spinning top sticking out of it, while her other hand supports a heavy book bag that probably weighs more than she does. She looks up at me and right away I can see by her expression that something is wrong.

"What's the matter?" I ask, relieving her of her hefty book bag. "You look unhappy."

"Oh, Jonah, we're soon to leave the Cape!" she cries. "Father has been reassigned to Rhode Island!"

Rachel places the wet bag on the floor and dams the tears in her eyes with her fingertips. "I thought for sure we'd be staying at least till June so I could finish the school year."

We both knew this day would come, but hearing it spoken aloud brings an instant lump to my throat. "Don't cry," I say, opening my arms so she can lay her head on my chest. "We'll think of something."

Mrs. Fernery, a math teacher, enters the lobby. From across the room, she spots me holding Rachel and separates us with the wagging of her finger and a stern look.

"What are we going to do?" Rachel asks, her woeful eyes looking to me for answers.

"I don't know. I suppose we will just have to keep in touch as best we can—-you know, telephone calls, letters. As soon as I have enough money saved, I'll take the train and come to visit."

A piece of fuzz from my wool sweater has stuck to her hair. Tenderly, I remove it and let it drop to the floor. "How soon will you be leaving?" I ask.

"In May—that's only two months from now! Oh, Jonah, I am sick over this! Even my mother doesn't want to go this soon. She adores the house we're renting, and she and my father have made some really nice friends here."

"Don't worry. If we put our heads together, we will find our way, Rachel—best friends always do."

She stands back and looks up at me. "Is that all I am to you, a best friend?" Her eyes fill again, this time spilling over.

"No, no, of course not—you are so much more to me than just a friend!" I pull the clean handkerchief from my trouser pocket and offer it to her. "I just said that because we tell each other everything. I don't quite know how it will be for me once you are gone. You are the only one who really understands me."

"And you are the only one who doesn't think of me as completely weird," Rachel says sheepishly, rewarding me with a faint smile.

The first period bell rings. I pick up the soggy brown bag and hand it to her so that I can carry both her book bag and mine. "Wait till you see what John and Barbara have done for their project," I tell her, trying to lift her mood. "They're going demonstrate Egyptian mummification."

I catch a glimpse of Alice Brighton heading in our direction and corral Rachel closer to the wall to avoid a run in, but it's too late. Alice has zeroed in on us. Smiling like the Cheshire cat, she hurries to block us at the base of the stairwell.

"Hello, Jonah," she drawls, twisting a lock of hair around one finger with a painted fingernail. She's wearing a tight black skirt and a pink cardigan sweater that looks like it would have fit my little sister four years ago.

"Hullo, Alice," I mumble, avoiding eye contact. "You'll have to excuse us; we're late for class." I nudge Rachel with my elbow, but she's too busy staring at the two marble-like bumps protruding from under Alice's sweater.

"Yeah," Alice scoffs, "I hear you two are giving a talk about some make-believe storm front you predict is supposedly going to hit Cape Cod."

"A storm of epic proportion would not restrict itself to the Cape; its damage would be widespread." Rachel corrects her, "Listen, we're now late, so would you mind stepping out of the way?"

"Don't let me hold you up, Ragamuffin," Alice counters, tucking one hand under my arm. "It's your boyfriend I want to speak to anyway, not you, so feel free to run along like a studious little girl."

"Cut it out, Alice!" I say, brushing her hand away as if it's a tarantula. Already I can feel the unease of a bad scene. I turn to Rachel. "We had better go."

Alice follows closely behind as we mount the stairs. At the top she says:—

"I just wanted to ask if you thought the shed job went as well as I thought it did. Mother has more work for you, if you've got time."

"Sorry," I say, over my shoulder, "someone else can do it."

"But would he be as good a kisser as you are? If you come, we could have a little hanky-panky replay."

Rachel stops short, her back ramrod straight. Alice's words have hit their mark. Rachel turns around to look at me; the expression on her face saying it all.

"What's the matter, *Ragamuffin,* didn't he tell you?" Alice's sneering voice bounces off the walls of the empty corridor.

"Rachel, I was going to tell you, I swear," but my excuse sounds pathetic.

Rachel must be processing the image of Alice and me alone in the shed, for all at once her face collapses into a theatrical mask of tragedy. She drops the bag she has been carrying, the noise echoing loudly, and takes off down the hall like a jackrabbit.

The commotion attracts the attention of my science teacher, Mr. Kellington, who comes out of his classroom to ask what the ruckus is all about.

"McFarley," he says, seizing me firmly by my collar, "what are you doing lingering in the hall?"

Pulling free of him, I pick up the top and the sodden brown bag and cast Alice a threatening look.

"Was that Miss Coulter I saw running down the hall? What happened? Where has she gone to?" Kellington demands.

"I'm afraid Rachel received some bad news, Mr. Kellington," Alice jokes. "She's probably halfway home by now."

"Shut up, Alice!" I yell.

"That will be enough, McFarley!" Kellington spats. "And you, Miss Brighton, why are you lingering in the hall? Return to your classroom this instant before you find yourself in detention for the week!"

Alice gives him a coquettish wink before turning to walk away, appearing as though she has all the time in the world.

Mr. Kellington gives me a shove toward the classroom. "You and Miss Coulter are dangerously close to receiving a failing grade for this project. She did not request permission to leave class; and you, young man, are now seriously late for it."

"Rachel had no time to ask for a pass, sir. She felt sick and has gone to the nurse," I lie. "With your permission, I will present our project to the class. Rachel and I have worked too hard to lose this grade. Please, sir."

Old Kellington considers me. "All right, McFarley, but you had better not be wasting my time. If you are the even the least bit unprepared—-and believe me, I will know if you are not fully prepared—-not only will I put a halt to your presentation, but I will issue you and Miss Coulter an *F* for your grades. Do I make myself clear?"

"Crystal clear, sir," I reply.

Forty pairs of eyes watch me enter the classroom with my arms full. I see some of them giving me their thumbs up; others are snickering.

I place Rachel's and my book bags on the floor and set the soggy bag containing the childish spinning top on the floor. I open our book bags and bring out all the paperwork Rachel so painstakingly worked on, not at all sure just how or where to begin. More than ever, I wish she was here. *Please, God, don't let him call on me first.*

Typical of the bad luck that followed me to school today, Old Kellington makes me to go first. I hear him bellow out my name; and as I make my way up the aisle with my arms full, I glance over to the classroom door in hopes that Rachel might have had a change of heart. It is no surprise to see she is not there.

I settle my papers on the podium in front of me and look out at my classmates. The intent faces show various levels of eager anticipation for the theory I am about to try to prove. I wonder how many would be supportive if they knew what a thief, liar, and scoundrel I've become.

What would they think of Jonah McFarley, the preacher's son, who— with the help of Alice Brighton's experienced tongue, has now sunk to an all-time low?

Frances

This languid morning finds me observing a pair of insectivorous Downy woodpeckers intent on extracting their morning meal from the aged hickory tree in my front yard. I watch the male as he quickly scours large areas of bark, pausing every few seconds to ensure that his tiny mate, recklessly hammering the tips of the bare branches beneath him, is having as much success as he in her own quest for food.

A fat gray squirrel comes to steal the show. He has scampered out from the shrubs, hopping across the lawn, to arrive near the base of the hickory tree. With his nose pressed to the ground, the pickings are few today; but he is smart enough to look up, where a few clinging nut pods have survived winter's ravaging and remain clinging to the tree's branches.

The squirrel leaps and lands squarely on the trunk of the tree, digging his claws into the hoary bark as he scurries up to claim his find. I think for sure that the woodpeckers will fly away, but they are reluctant to relinquish their good luck and merely flutter to the opposite side of the tree trunk.

I find it therapeutic to watch birds——to monitor how aptly they occupy the same space while sharing the common need for survival, thus warily making room for intruders. As with all nature's creatures, this woodpecker duo protects one another from the unexpected dangers of everyday existence, and I can't help but compare their well-suited companionship to that of Catherine and myself. So supportive of each other are we, I would even go so far as to say that had she not chosen to marry, I might have asked her to be my live-in companion.

Even after she admitted to her infelicitous behavior with Jack Wakefield, I still love Catherine with all my heart, though I cannot understand what possessed her to give in to that insidious rake, a man I never trusted and now detest. Catherine had said I was not to put the blame entirely on him, but he stands accused in my mind. Then again, who am I to judge anyone when I, myself, am guilty of sin?

My own demon screams out from deep inside my soul and rises up to strangle what little is left of my hardened heart. Its great head is *Jealousy*; its foreboding body, *Denial*. I can almost feel the demon bearing down on me, suffocating me, until I surrender to *Truth* and stand naked before it. But the demon still will not relent. It shrieks its ghastly condemnation, forcing me to address my own true feelings of love and yearning for a woman who can only ever be for me forbidden.

The stress of my reasoning is so all-consuming that I tremble under the weight of it. The demon of conscience grips me in its mighty fist, squeezing me tighter and tighter until I cannot breathe for the excruciating pain of it.

I slump over in my chair, any sensation of feeling now entirely gone from my left side. My mouth falls slack. I cannot see out of my left eye and the vision in my right is blurred.

The pain in my skull becomes so intense, I believe my guileless life to be waning; and only when I cry out with no more voice than an idiot's utterance does the demon consider releasing its fatal grip, making me believe it has left me for dead.

It seems an eternity that I am totally incapacitated, until finally there is a knock at my door—a light knock at first, then more insistent. Then, the knocking ceases. I begin to panic, fearing that whoever it was thought no one was home and left. My bladder releases on its own accord; were it not for the odor, I would not even realize it. Mortified, my eyes dart about wildly in my head. I try to calm myself, but I cannot think clearly.

Minutes later, I can hear the sound of a key being turned in the lock. I feel the draft as the front door is pushed open wide; and suddenly, help is by my side.

"Mrs. Gellermont! Mrs. Gellermont, can you hear me?"

The voice, strong and capable, is familiar to me, but I cannot place it. Shaking now, I try in vain to turn my head.

"It's me—Jonah McFarley!"

The blurred vision crouched low in front of me rises up and moves from sight. I feel the weight of my tapestry lap throw being tucked securely around my shivering body.

"Don't move, Mrs. Gellermont!" the voice instructs. *Whose voice is it? I can't remember,* and I feel a warm hand upon my shoulder.

"Stay calm, you hear? I'm going for help. I will be right back!" And with the slamming of the door, he is gone.

The temperature in the room warms, and I close my eyes to wait. In the silence that follows, it occurs to me that I am looking death in the face. *A vision appears. I am sitting in a great conference room, signing documents that have been placed before me.*

I have taken care of business.

I am ready should I be called to journey home.

Catherine

I have baked a batch of cranberry-orange muffins, thanks to a generous bag of berries from Margaret Malone's cranberry bog. I baked them for the church ladies who are paying Frances a visit on this gloomy day, but the tangy aroma of cranberry and orange has my family hovering around the table like ants near a sugar bowl. I whisk the three of them away, insisting the muffins must first cool and take a seat beside the table like a watchdog, reflecting on Frances and her condition.

In the eight weeks since the onset of her stroke, there has been a hired nurse and a regiment of neighbors and parishioners to help her. Edward and Blanche are resentful that their aunt prefers the care of her townspeople to that of the stodgy nursing home they had originally selected for her convalescence. I can't say as I blame my friend for refusing to go to Boston, with no one but her dolt of a nephew and his pregnant, overbearing wife to oversee her wellbeing. In fact, she had let me know, by means of guttural protest, that she would undoubtedly suffer another stroke if she were made to live with her Edward and Blanche.

As soon as I assured her that would not be the case, that Edward would have to take her over my dead body, the great lady put her trust in God (and me) and embarked on the road to recovery. Personally, I believe my home cooking to be the best remedy for her. Hearty meals and the everyday rhythm of an active family will help see her through her recuperation.

William insists on setting aside a portion of every day to assist Frances with her spiritual healing. In large part, he is doing it out of the goodness of his heart, though even William would admit he can be persuaded to air his biased opinions on political or economical issues with anyone willing to lend an ear. Frances, poor thing, is William's captive audience, though admittedly, Frances never turns away from verbal sparring. In fact, she finds it invigorating, despite her speech impediment.

Thankfully, William no longer sees her as a threat (not that she ever was), encouraging me instead to spend more time with her. This is all well and good except that my husband and I now see much less of each other as a result.

The doctors say Frances's recovery is going better than they had hoped. Not only has she been making great strides in regaining her mobility, but her speech therapist believes she will be speaking fluently again very soon now and will depend less on facial expressions to communicate. Still, it is plain to see that Frances and her needs have begun taking a toll on all of us.

I'm afraid to say that we McFarleys are a sorry-looking lot. In just a matter of weeks, two of us have aged, and all four of us are definitely leaner. It has been difficult taking on added responsibilities while keeping the hub of our own lives on track within what seems to be a shortage of hours in the day. Even our Lizzie, taking on the role of nursemaid, has had to become wiser beyond her years. I sometimes see her offer her 'Auntie Frances' a cool drink, encouraging her to grasp the paper straw though slackened lips. When Frances dribbles, Lizzie will take a clean napkin and tenderly dab the corners of her mouth. It saddens me to see my daughter exposed to life's realities at her young age.

Even Jonah has been doing more than his fair share to help out. It pleases me to see that he is not so self-absorbed that an invalid's helpless condition cannot evoke some sympathy in him. Whether he lends a hand because it was he who discovered Frances in her distress or because he and his girl have been estranged these past weeks, Jonah and Frances seem to have bonded in some extraordinary way.

Frances, who for as long as I have known her has never had more than a mild tolerance for children, is now a willing listener to my son's endless dialogue on the subject of his new obsession, the unchartered field of weather forecasting. They spend blocks of time conversing about this until either Frances shows signs of fatigue or Jonah has some chore to do. Other times I will see them share a simple visual exchange, like an unspoken bond between victim and savior, and I can tell that their connection is emotionally deeper than anything Frances and I have ever shared, or ever will.

A tantalizing citrus scent seeps through the cotton cloth I have draped over the basket of warm muffins. I don my coat and hat and stop to see William on my way out. He is in his office, trying to put on his coat, while Elizabeth droops distractedly over her homework assignment.

"I can fetch the mail, Father," she offers, "please let me."

"You would need your coat, and you're not done with your homework. Be a good girl and finish," he tells her, "and we'll have one of your mother's delicious muffins when you are done."

I shake my head. William talks to our daughter as if she was still a little child playing with her Flossie Flirt doll.

"I'll get the mail; I've already got my coat on."

I place the muffins on the stair and head for the door, but not before I catch my husband slyly slipping his hand through the rung of the banister and lifting a corner of the napkin to sniff the muffins.

"You will not disrupt that basket if you know what's good for you," I warn him. "I left extras in the kitchen for you and Lizzie. Be sure to save the third for Jonah."

I walk to the end of the driveway beneath an overcast sky. This is the dreariest season on the Cape, just before the birth of spring. The island is cast in a drab, misty wash of grays and browns.

I pull open the flap of our mailbox and reach inside to pull out several envelopes. Flipping through them as I make my way back to the house, I see a few bills; the rest are either advertisement flyers or church-related correspondence.

But wait! Hidden among the stack of white envelopes is one of ivory parchment, identical to that which I received six months prior, only this one was posted in Panama. My heart pounds as once again I recognize the familiar scrawl with *J.D.* penned in the upper left corner of the envelope.

Two fat rain drops splatter my face, and the promised shower begins to fall. I tuck Jack's letter in my pocket and hurry up to the porch to find William standing in the doorway. I feel my heart lurch to wonder how long he has been watching me.

"What arrived?"

I hand over the stack of envelopes. "Just some bills, it looks like, and a few advertisements."

"Nothing else?" he asks.

"No, it's all there," I say, feeling the color drain from my face as I watch him ruffling through the batch. "Were you expecting something?"

"Yes, I've been waiting for an estimate for the organ repair, which should have gotten here by now. I'll have to call again."

Preoccupied, William walks away, while I look out to a sky that is becoming increasingly darker. Jonah's science report comes to mind, and I wonder to myself: *could a hurricane be any worse than my husband's reaction should he discover that Jack has written to me yet again?*

Jonah

Don't ask how, but Mr. Kellington gave Rachel and me an *A* for our theory on hurricane forecasting. It probably would have been an *A*+ had Rachel herself been there, and if I had not been feeling every bit the dog for being untrue to a girl who deserves far better than the likes of me.

I take Rachel's hand in mine. It feels cool and lifeless. She hasn't gotten over what happened between me and Alice Brighton, and although she has agreed to come with me to the dance hall tonight, her icy expression warns me against showing her any affection.

The band is playing Bing Crosby's *I've Got a Pocketful of Dreams,* and the dance floor is getting crowded with dancers swaying to the catchy tune. We weave among the couples until we find a small clearing just off the dance floor. Our awkwardness feels like we have a wall between us. I'm afraid to hold Rachel's hand for fear she will shrug me off.

The remaining days on the Cape are swiftly down for the Coulters, which makes me wish all the more that I could hold Rachel close. At least I see that she is wearing the sand dollar necklace I gave to last Valentine's Day. If she despised me as much as I worry she might, I doubt she would be wearing it. It pleases me to see her keep reaching up to gently run a finger over the shell, as if it contained some sort of magical powers.

It had been the best shell in my entire collection. I found it years ago at Newcomb's Hollow, the backshore of Wellfleet. It was the day after a small nor'easter had come through and the ocean had disgorged a fair amount of sand dollars, most of them chipped, stained or broken.

My friends and I found a number of them that day, but this was the only nice-sized one that was whole. It was dingy, but flat and round as a circle. I brought it home and soaked it in a solution of water and bleach until it turned white. My father had long ago told me the legend of the sand dollar, which I remember telling Rachel the day I gave her my gift.

"The holes commemorate the five wounds of Christ, and the etched flower on one side is the Easter lily, with its heart the Star of Bethlehem," I had told her. "And on the other side is an etched Christmas poinsettia, which is supposed to be a reminder of Christ's birth." I watched Rachel's eyes grow wide, and the corners of her mouth turn up until she displayed a smile which seemed to take up her entire face. "That's not all. If you shake a sand dollar gently, you can hear the little shell doves inside." I shook the shell beside her ear. Sure enough, we could hear the tiny shell doves rattling around inside.

As soon as the band stops playing, I lead Rachel out to the lobby, where patrons are smoking and purchasing refreshments. I pull a pack of cigarettes from my jacket pocket, tap it against my palm to expose the ends, and offer it first to Rachel. She surprises me by taking one. I remove another for myself and strike a match. We inhale, standing in stony silence, each with our own thoughts swirling around our heads as thick as the smoke.

Not speaking seems a huge waste of time that neither of us has to spare. The Coulters will soon be leaving for Rhode Island, but I feel like the only one who is aware of just how fast these weeks are going to fly by.

Bending over to grind the stub of my cigarette in a nearby ashtray, I look up to find Rachel scrutinizing me. The hurt I see in her eyes feels worse than any punishment.

"Rachel, I can't tell you enough times how really sorry I am," I tell her.

"I suppose you want me to forgive you?" she baits.

"Don't make me crawl."

"Why shouldn't I?" she asks. "You're a snake——a sneaky, slithering snake."

"I'm sorry for hurting you and for my behavior with Alice. I was a cad! It was horribly stupid of me, and I am sick for having broken your heart. Tell me what can I say or do to make it up to you?" I beg. "I want to make things better between us. It's bad enough that you're leaving without our having bad feelings between us when you go. Please, Rachel."

"I am not sure I am capable of forgiving you. It isn't bad enough you broke my heart? Now you and that...that *floozy* have made a mockery of me in school," Rachel says, her voice breaking.

The fact that she is right, and that I am powerless to turn back time, has me hanging my head in shame.

"I think when the time comes to leave for Rhode Island, it would be best if you and I just say goodbye," she suggests, ignoring my defense. "You were my first friend, Jonah; we had great times together, but obviously we view things—important things—very differently."

"Rachel, you know that's untrue! Listen, we can make this work, in spite of what happened and in spite of the separation of miles. You have your sights set on college; and just like your parents, you are going to be a great meteorologist someday. I plan to join the Navy, whether America goes to war or not. When I have served my time, your father said he'd help me get into a meteorological program. Like you, I believe there is a tremendous need for forecasting. We've both got some growing up to do, but we can have a future together, if both of us want it badly enough. Rachel, I love you, and I believe you love me, too."

"I do love you, Jonah, but there is more to it," Rachel says, softening.

"No, there's not! We just have to stay focused." I grasp her hands in mine. "We need to stay focused and realize we are heading in the same direction."

I can almost see Rachel weighs my words. Finally, she gives me a little nod.

"All right, I'll give you one more chance. But let me tell you, buster, if ever I find out that you so much as *look* at, much less touch, Alice Brighton again, I'll—"

I pull her to me, cutting off the rest of her threat with a kiss. I murmur sweet nothings with my lips against her hair and feel her relax, believing that this time I won't let her down.

She pulls back to look up at me through dreamy, half-lidded eyes. "Maybe this is what the astrologers mean when they talk about the stars *aligning.*"

I bend over to kiss my girl again. But this time, our kiss lasts a lot longer.

Frances

It took a near-death experience to redefine my appreciation for living. When I suffered the stroke I thought for sure my time had come, but apparently the Lord has work for me yet to do.

I must have been a disappointment to our funeral director, the morose Benjamin Fromlehide, who came to visit me soon after my debilitation. His oily overtures and morbid bouquet of white gladiolas, undoubtedly leftover from a previous funeral, made me think he could already hear the bells tolling for me.

I envisioned him on his drive over making a mental measurement for my casket. If he had hoped to line his pockets with the benefit of my demise, imagine his surprise to discover me seated in my parlor, dressed as a sovereign in a silk brocade dressing gown, surrounded by a group of community ladies in waiting.

Having him find me thus was one of my better moments. Many times after that proved to be devastatingly difficult as I fought for months to regain my strength. With every earnest try, defeat was there to challenge and discourage me, and I became acutely aware of the possibility that I could end up little more than a shadow of my former self.

By the end of the second month of rehabilitation, I had relearned nearly all of my motor skills but could progress no further with speech therapy. The therapist who had been working on my case recommended I enter the Lahey Clinic, in Boston, to see what more could be done for me. Desperate to make a full recovery, I enrolled at the clinic at the end of April. It was here, at Lahey, that I was fortunate enough to befriend Harriet Langley, another stroke victim like myself.

Harriet and her sense of humor saved me when I first arrived depressed and homesick. She is a jovial gal, who smokes like a chimney whenever she can sneak a cigarette, and finds good in everyone and everything. Her mantra is never to take life too seriously.

It is because of Harriet that I overcame my fears and inhibitions. Together we have vaulted through the grueling and tedious exercise regime, regulating our respiration, practicing our vowels and consonants, and reading aloud while simultaneously timing our breathing so that we *inspire* properly when we speak. It is a mundane routine, these therapy sessions, but Harriet's positive outlook on life carries us over the hump each and every time, and we have shared many a joke at the expense of our wonderful therapists and nurses.

She is related, I came to find out, to the renowned scientist, Doctor Jeremy Sims, whose name is familiarly associated with the *NFIP*. He is Harriet's brother-in-law, former recipient of the prestigious *Dalsborg Chemistry Award*, bestowed on him for his outstanding achievement in the field of science, with particular emphasis on infantile paralysis. He and his wife, Davina, have visited Harriet on several occasions while I've been here. Their staunch belief in our recovery helps us to overcome the verbal obstacles that have, until now, prevented us from acquiring near-perfect diction and enunciation.

It is a pleasant surprise that young Dr. Sims should happen by on the day I am to leave the clinic. He appears mid-morning, in the doorway to my room, his hat and coat in hand, inquiring after my health. Even though his query is friendly enough, I feel the unease of inadequacy between us. I feel I am at a disadvantage, for there have been few occasions when we have exchanged but a few pleasantries. The difference in our cerebral intelligence unnerves me, so sure am I that Dr. Sims is accustomed to a far higher level of conversation.

I invite him to join me and, surprisingly, he accepts, pulling the extra chair in the room closer to mine. His slight built, with a disheveled style of dressing, somehow becomes him; and his face, which is twisted with an appealing expression of analytical perplexity, appears as though he is trying to solve all the scientific problems of the world.

"How unfortunate you missed the t-tea cart by a mere half hour," I say, hearing myself trip on a word. Though I am curious as to why he has come, nevertheless I am pleased to see him.

Undoubtedly, his celebrated presence makes me feel self-conscious, but I set my nervousness aside for the chance to share a segment of time with such a brilliant, contributing individual.

"I can only stay but a minute; Harriet is expecting me," he says, using his finger to push his wire-rimmed spectacles higher up the bridge of his nose. He eyes my portmanteau on the bed. "You must be very excited to be going home."

"Indeed! Though I shall miss the friends I have made here; namely, Harriet—and you, of course, Dr. Sims!"

"Please, won't you call me Jeremy?"

"I will, if you will call me F-Frances from now on."

The hum of incessant rain draws our attention as the opening topic of conversation. According to Catherine's letters, the weather has been *the ruination of tourism on the Cape so far this summer."*

"It is unfortunate that you must travel home on an unpleasant day such as this. Perhaps the sun is simply awaiting your return before shining again."

"If that were only the case...Jeremy," I blush. "My friends write the w-weather has been...dreadful this summer. I am told it has been...either hot and scorching, or w-wet and soggy."

"It's true," the doctor says. "You missed very little back home. There has been an unfortunate breakout of mold everywhere; our house staff has beside themselves trying to manage the mildew." He shifts in his seat.

"The summer weather is impossible to predict," I tell him.

"Yes, indeed," Dr. Sims agrees, "which is why my wife and I have chosen the agreeable month of September to host the *NFIP* fund raiser at our summer house, in Westhampton—September twenty-first, to be exact."

He pulls down on the corners of his vest, affording me a partial glimpse of a handsome pocket watch and chain.

"I have come to informally invite you; a proper invitation will, of course, be forthcoming," he says. "If you think you might enjoy such an event, Davina and I would insist on sending our driver for you. Since it is an exhausting trip, we would insist that you to spend the weekend, along with Harriet, as our guests." He blushes. "I assume you are familiar with the *March of Dimes?"*

"I am, of course," I assure him. "As you can guess, it is a cause m-most important to me."

"Then you must join us; it will be great fun! Harriet would be pleased for the company of a close friend. She battles against attending any social gathering alone and usually concocts some clever excuse to wheedle out of them. Unfortunately, her sister is hosting this one; therefore, Harriet can hardly refuse."

"I thank you for the invitation, but the d-date is three months off. If I am feeling well enough by that time, I will attend. If not, you may certainly expect to receive my check in the mail."

"We cannot accept your generosity unless it is hand-delivered, at which point you must take advantage of all the Hamptons have to offer by agreeing to spend a few days with us."

"We shall see. M-my nephew, Edward, and his wife are expecting a baby that very month. The child is to be my namesake. C-can you imagine? Assuming all goes well with the birth, you can count on seeing me."

Dr. Sims, whose face still appears as a mask of bewilderment, nods approvingly. "Good, it is settled then."

"Actually, Edward and his wife are on their way from Boston. They are c-coming to drive me home. This nasty weather is b-bound to deter them. I suggested Blanche not make the trip, but she has never been one to t-take anyone's advice, most especially mine."

I once knew a girl whose eyes opened round as saucers when she became frightened. Miss Scott, the Staff Director at Lahey, enters without knocking and interrupts my conversation with Dr. Sims. Her eyes have that same look about them.

"Excuse me, Mrs. Gellermont; Dr. Sims," she nods, "but I'm afraid I have some bad news." She comes to stand beside me and leans over. In a whisper she tells me, "We have just received a call saying your nephew, Edward, has been involved in an automobile accident."

"Edward? Tell me, are they are all r-right?" The room begins to spin and suddenly Jeremy is crouching beside me.

"Breathe, Frances," he coaches, chafing both my hands in his, "just breathe."

"Yes, m'am," the nurse assures me, "your nephew is fine, except for minor lacerations and being badly bruised. We are told it's his wife who suffered the worst of it."

"Blanche?" I cry, suddenly alarmed.

"Yes, M'am, I'm afraid so." Miss Scott pours a small amount of water into a glass and hands it to me. "They have taken her to the hospital. She's in labor."

Catherine

The SS Anchorage
Panama, June 20, 1938

Cat,
Our voyage from Alaska to Panama was uneventful. The seas
have been in our favor, enabling us to complete all stops
along the way. The ship will remain here in port until it has
been overhauled and repairs completed. I have chartered a
small fishing boat from a local sea captain. Two friends and I
will set sail for New England at the end of August. Panama
natives claim they can smell a storm brewing and warn us of
unusual activity near the Cape Verdes Islands, off the coast of
Africa. I'm not concerned, so don't you be; most of them are
no more than anglers, who couldn't catch a fish in a bucket.
My calculations have us arriving mid-day, on Wednesday,
September twenty-first, at Wings Neck. In the event our
arrival should be delayed, don't fear I had a change of heart.
My course has been set, and no winds will alter it.

Ever yours,
Jack

Being young, fanciful, and naive about lovemaking, any fantasy of what my first sexual encounter would be like was heavily laced with romantic notions. I would envision myself the very essence of femininity, looking my particular best, completely irresistible to my lover.

In the imaginary mind of a whimsical girl, her initial experience with lovemaking would never happen when or how it actually did. For who would have entertained a single romantic thought after a physically challenging day at the docks, raking dead fish, and reeking to high heaven? Jack, who was forever bringing out the tomboy in me, could not resist me on just such a day, so that the memory of my lost virginity will forever be emblazoned in my mind.

"C'mon, kid," Jack says, handing me a rake and fitting me with a pair of rubber boots. "I'm taking you to the docks."

It is a late August afternoon. The warming rays of the setting sun have cast the island in an amber glow and sparkle upon the water as brightly lit as yellow diamonds. We squint against the sun and gaze out to sea just in time to watch the little fleet of fishing boats heading for home.

A pair of playful harbor seals and several thieving herring gulls buoy in the water beneath the dock. Instinctively, they await the leftover ration of bait to be thrown overboard when the vessels' coolers are emptied of their catch.

The boats begin to file in, each engine slowing to a grumbling hum as its captain expertly maneuvers his craft dockside with the accuracy of a marksman. Brawny crewmen hurl thick roping from the decks, then hop agilely onto the dock to secure their vessel, using nautical knots passed down to them by previous generations of sailors.

Jack and I brace ourselves, our feet apart, beside the great metal chute and administer our rakes to help transfer the heavy poundage of seafood being systematically unloaded. The vacant eyes of dead fish—flounder, cod, sea bass, sole, and mackerel—slide by us in ghostly eeriness as we help move the pungent mounds so they can be slid down the slimy steel gurney to tumble, like a waterfall, into cavernous catch bins below.

The muscles of our arms and backs are near straining for the hour it takes us to finish the job. One of the fishermen passes each of us an ice cold bottle of beer to quench our thirst. We drink, propped up by our rakes, afraid to sit lest we never rise up again.

The evening hour brings the itchy bite of mosquitoes—those seasonal pests that leave behind telltale welts on our exposed skin and cleverly dodge our swatting hands as they circle our heads with their erratic, annoying buzzing. Jack's hair is matted against his forehead; my own is held back with a length of red grosgrain ribbon. Dark stains of perspiration pattern our shirts, testimonials to our hard labor. For months our skin has been branded by the summer sun. Now our vibrant health is more than evident in the flush of our faces.

Jack raises his beer bottle to me in a mock toast and gives me a smile weighted with seduction. It starts my heart racing, and I lean against the wooden rail for support. My heart pounds to where I can swear he must be able to see it pumping beneath my shirt. He cocks his head to one side as if appraising a piece of fine art and casts me a look of quizzical fascination. After what I have accomplished today, perhaps he is viewing me not just as an ordinary girl but as a woman capable of holding her own. Inwardly I preen with self confidence, for as always nothing means more to me than Jack's approval. I feel the livewire of desire spark like static electricity between us. It overrides the stench of raw fish just as thoroughly as our youth makes us oblivious to our shabby hygiene.

We finish our beer, step out of the rubber boots, and change back into our shoes. Jack takes my hand and we jump down off the dock, warding off the tips his father's fishermen friends hand us with gratitude. When we are out of earshot, Jack tells me he is taking me to his most secret hideaway. I nod in agreement, unsure of just where we are going, and nibble at my bottom lip while he leads the way. I quiver with anticipation as we cross the road and trespass across several properties. To conserve the last of our energy, we keep conversation between us minimal.

I think surely we have walked the entire length of the island as Jack leads me along winding passages of shrubbery that seemingly lead nowhere. But eventually we break through the woods and onto the warm sand of a secluded nook he has kept a secret until now. I cannot even remotely guess where we are, though I can tell it is somewhere on the bay side. The fact that Jack could bring us here so directly is testimony to his navigational skills, which he knows I always trust and never question.

Since both of us know exactly why we came, we begin shedding our clothes. Shyly, I turn away from him. When I am naked, I pull the red *ribbon from my hair and drop it on my dirty clothes, but the wind lifts the weightless trim like a long red kite tail, carrying it out to sea. Jack gives a tribal shout, taking off after it. I watch him jump up to snatch the ribbon from the air before it hits the water and marvel at the grace of his muscular body. To my mind, he is a nubile god. Breathlessly, Jack returns and hastily secures the ribbon into the pocket of his dirty shirt before grabbing my hand and pulling me, at a run, into the sea.*

We hit the water full force, plunging into its bracing surface, and emerge scrubbed clean by the molecular power of sand and salt. Wiping the water from my face, I believe I see a fleeting shadow of doubt flicker across Jack's brow. Before he can pose it as a question of honor, I fasten my mouth to assure him of my acquiescence in whatever it is we are about to do. It is important that he believes I am surrendering my body to him of my own free will.

His hold on me tightens, and I wrap my legs wantonly around his slender hips, folding my arms about his neck. We buoy this way, bobbing as one, over the rolling hump of the timely breaker waves. The motion is so rhythmic and similar to the actual act of lovemaking, that when Jack finally enters me, our mating is as effortless and transitional as breathing. We ebb and flow against one another, gently at first and then more intensely until both of us have crested, and we cry out our ecstasies as vocal as a pair of mating gulls.

When Jack's hardness subsides and he is no longer inside me, I feel the excess of his seed escape from my passage to blend with a living sea, which for centuries has witnessed ancient life forms reproducing and manifesting themselves.

When William rescued me from public shame, he insisted I tell him how many times Jack and I had coupled. I lied and said it had only been one time, when in truth we had made love on that isolated beach as often as we could manage to steal away during that hot, lazy summer.

Admittedly, I am unskilled in the way of deception, and William is much smarter than I credit him for. I suspect that, compared to what I was physically experiencing with Jack back then, my lack of affection toward my husband has much to do with our now lusterless marriage. Even today, I waste too much time fantasizing about the past, wondering how differently my life would have turned out if Jack had never left the island, convinced ours would have been a glorious union had he stayed rather than sailed away. I still view

Jack through rose-colored glasses, where William I see through dark, shaded ones. To no avail, I am forever singling out William's faults. I have to wonder what is to be gained by doing that.

I turn the car key in the ignition and begin heading back, the hypnotic motion of the windshield wipers taking me back to the year Mother died and a family friend suggested to my father we get a dog to help us through the grieving process...

Father and I went to the pound and chose a shaggy mutt we named Bogart, who possessed an inherited wild streak.

The dog wreaked havoc with our belongings and repeatedly relieved himself on every carpet in the house. Father quickly began to regret his purchase; and I, fearful he would return Bogart to the pound, asked if looking after a willful pet was any more taxing than the long hours we devoted to Mother when she was too ill to care for herself. My father thought the simplistic comparison quite clever on my part. He pondered this while Bogart obediently sat beside him, as if he knew Father was deciding his fate. I recall my father's eyebrows arching, and him nodding slowly. The curvature of his lips pressed together, and the thought devoted to his answer proved to me that my question had been a fair one.

"Catherine," Father said, mindlessly administering a playful rub upon Bogart's shaggy head, "if I have learned little else in all the years of living, I have learned that in life we merely trade one set of problems for another."

I shall be late in arriving at Frances's house with my basket of cold muffins. Still, I teeter along in no rush, recalling my father's remark, comparing it to my own expectations of love and the candidates of my heart—undoubtedly, Jack Wakefield and William McFarley.

Jonah

I've never been there, but I've heard the humidity in New Orleans is so bad in summer that walking in the streets is like walking through a body of water. That's the kind of humidity we've had on the Cape this summer.

Mother has offered to drive Aunt Frances (as Lizzie and I have been asked to call her) to Boston for an overnight visit to meet her newly-born great-niece. As if my life is not unhappy enough now that Rachel has left for Rhode Island, my relationship with my mother has been tense, especially since announcing enlistment into the Navy. I leave at the end of September following the anticipated visit from the infamous Jack Wakefield.

My mother may have been feeling the need to get away and used the Boston trip as her excuse. Nevertheless, she is gone for an overnight, and I am left with the disagreeable job of managing my sister and putting dinner on the table. *How hard can it be to arrange a cold platter?* Tuna salad on a few lettuce leaves, hardboiled eggs, cold peas and tomato wedges. With little air movement to be had, no one craves a hot meal, and everybody's nerves seem as raw as a side of beef.

My sister shuffles barefoot into the kitchen, looking limp as a dishrag and noisily chewing a wad of bubblegum. She slouches against my shoulder, her skin as sticky as fly paper; I shrug her off irritably. She eyes what I'm laying out for supper and makes a face.

"I don't want tuna salad," she whines.

"We're ready to eat. Pour your milk and tell Father we're ready," I say.

"I want Kool-Aid," she demands, masterfully extending her lips and producing a bubble from her gum the size of a grapefruit.

I have no doubt that if Mother was here my sister would be made to drink milk; but I'm hot and irritable, so I give Lizzie her way.

"Have what you like," I tell her, "but don't use any ice—we haven't enough to spare. Now go tell Father that dinner is ready."

"FA-TH-H-ER, DIN-NER!" she bellows from where she stands.

"Not like that—you sound like a fishwife! The windows are open!" I pull her by one of her clammy arms and wrestle her into her chair.

"Well, Elizabeth," Father says, entering the kitchen and taking his seat at the head of the table, "I think all our neighbors heard that call to supper."

Father pinches the bridge of his nose the way he does when he feels one of his headaches coming on. He is not used to Mother being away or not having the car at his disposal. There are two purple stains of fatigue under his eyes, and his shirt is opened with the sleeves rolled up. He appears done in, and I think it's no wonder. He is a man who has always carried the weight of the world, and this last year that burden has gotten much heavier.

I put the platter in the center of the table and wait for our father to say grace. He drags the back of one hand across his forehead then joins both hands together. It never fails to move me when I look at my father's immaculate hands, with their handsomely-veined fingers, intertwining to form the familiar clerical position for prayer. He says:—

"Bless us, Lord, and thy bounty before us, which we have because of your goodness and benevolence—"

"A-men," we answer in unison.

Lizzie slumps further in her chair while I fix her a plate. "Just the egg and a few peas," she orders. "No tuna. I won't eat it."

"You will eat what is put before you," Father tells her.

Lizzie sits up straight and defiantly folds her arms across her chest. Her eyebrows form a small *w*. Clearly she is displeased at having been corrected twice by the one person who seldom finds fault with anything she says or does. She picks up a wedge of egg with her fingers and pops it into her mouth, then proceeds to idly push her peas around on the plate with her fork until several of them roll off the plate and onto the table.

Without Mother here to keep the conversational ball rolling, the silence is deep enough that we can hear each other chewing. I break it by addressing the 'elephant in the room,' so to speak.

132

"Have you and Mother forgiven me?" I ask my father.

"You have done nothing that requires forgiveness. Joining the armed forces and serving one's country is an honorable thing, after all."

"And yet, you didn't choose it for yourself."

"No, I did not. However, my father served. He was in the infantry during the First World War. I was twelve when he left, sixteen when he returned home. Those were hard times for our family," he recalls. "Had she not had a family to care for, I believe my mother would have died of loneliness. I vowed that if and when God gave me children, unless there was a military draft I would be there to watch them grow up."

"I'm growing up, though no one wants to let me," Lizzie mutters. She drains the last of her Kool-Aid and sits sulking, her top lip red-rimmed with food coloring.

"You are, indeed," Father says, "but you will grow stronger and faster if you eat your dinner." He fills her fork with food and makes her take it. "There are starving children in other countries with not a morsel to eat, you know."

"You're not eating," Lizzie points out.

"You're right." Obediently my Father opens his mouth quickly deposits a forkful of food.

I poke her in the arm and tell her to help me clear the dishes. Only when she has finished drying them do I let her have a chocolate brownie from the batch Mother left for us. Lizzie takes it like a thief and hurries out the screen door in search of her girlfriend next door.

Father shakes his head. "It's beastly hot in here, isn't it? It's cooler outside. Want to join me for a smoke out on the porch?" He sees the look on my face and shrugs his shoulders. "I figure it's high time I start treating you like a man—you'll be one soon enough."

Outside is really no cooler, but we sit side by side in the porch rockers. Father taps two cigarettes from the pack in his pocket and strikes a match. Lighting his first, he holds the matchstick up to mine. I try not to look as comfortable as I am with a cigarette in my mouth, inhaling deeply and taking in the shared moment. We sit, quietly observing Lizzie and her friend, Margaret, playing a game of hopscotch on the sidewalk.

Every few minutes we flail our arms at the hungry mosquitoes, smacking those which have found their fleshy marks, punctured, and drawn blood. The exhale of smoke seems to ward them off somewhat, so I blow a few smoke rings and watch most of them retreat and disappear as quickly as they came. Father seems surprised I can do that.

"How do you feel about meeting Jack Wakefield?" he asks. "The day is almost here."

I shrug my shoulders. "I don't know; I'm not nervous, if that's what you mean."

"That's good. I'm going to insist your mother stay behind that day. You're old enough to drive yourself to meet his boat."

Taking the car out alone is enticing, but the thought of meeting the man who fathered me falls just short of terrifying. I had figured Mother could be the buffer who helps pave the way between me and some total stranger.

Sensing my reluctance, Father tells me:—

"You have nothing to worry about. In his own way, Jack Wakefield is a good enough man." He inhales the last of his cigarette and stubs it out on the bottom of his shoe, flicking the butt with one finger so it sails over the porch railing and disappears in the garden. "If anyone is nervous on that day, it will be me."

"Why?" I ask.

"I'm afraid of losing you to him," my father says.

The tinkling bells of the white Good Humor truck interrupts us as it slowly turns onto our street. Children and parents suddenly appear out of nowhere to gather at the corner.

As Lizzie bounds up the porch steps, Father is already reaching into his pocket for loose change and hands her two coins.

"Here—treat yourself and Margaret," Father tells her, "and you may keep the change."

Lizzie closes her fingers around the money as fast as a Venus flytrap can catch a fly and throws him a look not unlike our Mother does when she has gotten her way.

"You're super keen!" she says, thanking Father with a noisy kiss upon his cheek. "Do you want an ice cream bar, Jonah?" she asks, probably hoping I won't so she can keep the change.

I shake my head. After sharing a smoke with my father, eating an ice cream seems juvenile. "I'm fine, thanks."

Lizzie dances down the steps to join Margaret, and I call out to her:—

"Come back when you're done! It'll be time for your bath!"

"You are very much your mother," Father observes.

"I am you, too," I assure him kindly, "and I have always needed you. I suspect the reasons *why* may change over time, but the *how much* never will."

Frances

From the look of the stack of clothing on my bed, one would think I was going abroad rather than spending just three days in the Hamptons, but better to have too many outfits than too few. Except for my lingerie, which I like to choose for myself, Mary has laid out everything I will need. There are lighter, more airy dresses for daytime and dressier ones for evening attire. Before leaving she took care to position my antique jewelry armoire beside the bed and has left the key to it in plain view. Simply put, Mary organizes my life.

When Bentley was alive, we kept a social calendar. Back then, I had occasion to wear all the jewelry I own, which will one day be passed down to my great-niece and namesake, baby Frances. My nephew could be trusted to safeguard it until Frances is of age, but I fear his self-serving wife would sell it all, given the chance. To ensure against that ever happening, I have delegated the collection be kept in Trust for the baby, per my specific instruction.

It is a tiresome assignment to select jewelry, and while I am sifting quickly among a few of the more weighty pieces, I gouge my forefinger on the end of a stick pin and wince sharply from the sting of it. Instantly, a dot of blood appears at the site and spreads. I smile ruefully to see it is not blue, as Bentley believed ours to be; neither is it black, as my good conscience would dictate it ought to be. Alas, my blood is simply red, just like anyone else's.

I squeeze below the wound to encourage flow and lower my lips to it while I locate the tube of ointment and an adhesive bandage from the medicine cabinet in the bathroom. Hobbling back to the bedroom I find Catherine waiting. So silently did she enter that for a moment I think I imagine her there.

"I see you have decided to accept the invitation from Dr. and Mrs. Sims," she says, eyeing the finery on the bed.

"I suppose I have," I reply, welcoming her feather-like kiss upon my cheek. "After another one of those exasperating overnight visits with Edward and Blanche, all of which from now on will include the hoopla of one soon-to-be-spoiled little girl, I am more than ready to relax with the Sims and blend with Westhampton's upper crust." I motion her toward a boudoir chair. "How is it you have found time to visit me so close to dinner time?"

"Everyone at home is preoccupied, and I'm feeling blue," she admits.

"Do join me then. I could use your keen eye to help me with accessory choices." Swiftly, I free my arms of the crutches and sit on the edge of my bed.

Catherine shimmies to the edge of the cushion, opens the chest and peers at its contents with the fascination of a little girl playing at dressing up. Her eyes are as round as saucers; in the depths of her pupils I can spot the reflection of shimmering gold, polished silver, and brilliant gemstones.

"Be careful with the brooches," I warn her, "I've just received a nasty prick from one of the pins." I hold up my bandaged finger as proof, but she pays me no mind. Her hands are fluttering over the jewels like butterflies above brightly-colored flowers. Finally she dips in to pick up a large cameo and gently traces the face of the ivory silhouette with her fingertip.

"This lovely piece is familiar," she says. "I have admired it on you on many a holiday. It belonged to your grandmother, did it not?

"It was my *great*-grandmother's, on my mother's side—Rebecca Pierpont. I was often told growing up that it was her willful ways and stubbornness I inherited."

She carefully sets aside the valuable antique and reaches for another trinket, this time an enamel crown set in platinum, decorated with tiny diamonds and seed pearls.

"That was a gift from Bentley. He bought it for me the year we rented a villa on the Cote d'Azur, along the French Riviera. It is from the Belle Époque collection—Belle Époque meaning *Beautiful Era*. The jewelry was very much in demand twenty years ago; now I find it rather gaudy. " I lightly trace a fingertip around the crown's perimeter. "Notice the lacy filigree and the knife-edge setting? They are typical design traits of the Époque style."

Catherine replaces this piece to its safekeeping and sighs heavily. I imagine she has had enough of admiring riches beyond what she could ever dream of affording, though she has never held it against me for being born wealthy.

She yawns, and stretches her arms over her head, signaling her inquisition of my jewelry is over except for choosing a few appropriate ornamental matches for my Hampton weekend. I have long valued her accurate eye for couture and now watch amusedly as Catherine sits back down and knowingly begins matching accessories to outfits.

Since it is my trip, I should not sit idly while my friend makes what ought to be my own choices. I pick up my crutches and move to the dresser where I lean them against the wall and pull open the top drawer by its two weighty brass fixtures. A faint waft of Chanel No. 5 greets me, making it a pleasant task to pick and choose among a folded assortment of pale, satiny undergarments and flesh-colored hosiery. I select what I think I will need to take with me and set them all aside.

Though my back is to her, I can see Catherine's reflection in the mirror above my bureau. Her chin is lowered, but I catch a glimpse of her mouth, sulkily twisted to one side, while she busies herself with her preoccupation. Neither of us has yet to mention the arrival of Jack Wakefield, who is due to sail in to port in less than a week's time. I sigh wistfully, thinking it unfair of me to call upon my friend to help me pack without encouraging her to unburden whatever is weighing so heavily on her mind. She is as quiet as a church mouse. I keep my own head bent to my task and inquire lightly:—

"Do you think Jonah is ready for next week?" We both know exactly to what I am referring.

"He appears indifferent, but I can tell he's torn," she admits. "Part of him is more than curious about meeting Jack, but I think he is afraid that he might actually *like* him. Naturally, this would pain him, since clearly his loyalties lie with William."

"Ha! As if that vagabond, Jack Wakefield, could ever hold a candle to the likes of William McFarley," I say.

"Please don't make assumptions, Frances. You know nothing of the man other than that which you have heard from me or from idle gossip in town. Jack is, after all, Jonah's real father."

I whip around at this stupidity, nearly losing my balance. "He is m-most certainly *not!*" I stammer, holding the bedpost as I teeter on my feet. "Why, William has raised that boy! It is he who has taught Jonah all that a father should about family values, self-esteem, and honor. If being a father is to love

137

and protect, then William is Jonah's father in every sense of the word." I relax some and let go of the post, embarrassed at my own outburst. "You know every bit I say is true, Catherine."

Wearily I drop down onto a corner of the bed. Even a tirade as small as this can leave me winded nowadays. My constitution is no longer as strong as it once was.

"Of course, you are right," Catherine agrees, no doubt noticing how my lecture took its toll on me.

She moves a stack of dresses so as to sit beside me and strokes my hand for a moment. We can feel the air in the room move for the first time in hours. It is only a quick little cross breeze that enters through the open windows, teases the curtains, and passes over so quickly that I wonder if I was merely wishing for it.

"I was not speaking literally," Catherine says. "No other man could have been half the father William has been to Jonah. Not a day goes by that I don't remember how William was there for me. From the very first, he has been there for me and our family—and every day since."

"If that is true, and you believe you have a decent man in William, why then do you appear so forlorn?"

"I want to be there when Jack sets his eyes on Jonah for the first time." She hangs her head and whispers, "God forgive me, but I want so much to see him! After all these years of dreaming about him—wondering where he's been, places he has seen—I believe I deserve that much, regardless of the fact that..."

"William forbids it?" I finish for her. "Who can blame him? He has watched you bloom like a rose this past year. We all have seen it. You have blossomed despite a troubled world, the declining health of your most trusted friend, the heartache of your son leaving for the military, and the demands of young daughter in need of her mother's attention." I feel the familiar bile of jealousy rising in my throat.

"Exactly what is it that you are you implying?" Catherine asks me.

"I do not imply; I am merely stating fact. You have maintained your looks in spite of all the odds. How is that, I should like to know? Or should I ask *who* are you doing it for? Has all your strength of character been only to impress the notorious Jack Wakefield?"

"No, of course not," she lies.

"Humph! Jack Wakefield! He gave you nothing but a few sweaty humps, filled your belly with his seed, and then sailed away from his responsibilities.

He didn't care enough to make an honest woman of you or to make provision for the son you were bearing him."

"It wasn't like that," Catherine strikes out, getting up from the bed to stand accused. "There was so much good in him, so much that no one saw but me. I still want to see him! I need to see him! You of all people should understand—you, my closest, dearest friend!"

Catherine's forehead falls into her hands. A sob of defeat escapes her, and she says miserably, "There was so much more to him than what you think you know."

"I do not doubt there is. But tell me—what good can possibly come of obsessing over a man, who not only does not deserve you, but whom you can never be with? I am asking you to be realistic."

When she raises her head to me, her beautiful features are twisted, riddled with grief. "I live with reality every day, and it's cold. Sometimes I long for the warmth of fantasy."

"We all do," I admit, "but fantasy is only the creative power of your imagination at work, whereby to live in reality is to exist in the here and now."

Catherine's shoulders slump with the weight of her sorrow and my words. I feel the onset of my own unrequited love, and bereavement presses full on my chest.

When she looks up, Catherine says, "It seems all those I love the most are leaving me, one by one."

"That is not true. Why, Jonah doesn't leave for another few weeks, and I shall only be gone a few days. Besides, you always have William and Elizabeth—they both are here for you. William will always be here for you."

"That he will, but it's not the same," she replies. "How am I to fill the void of emptiness I feel in my heart? It's an emptiness which will be even more pronounced once Jonah leaves home."

Whether it is the difference in our ages or my intolerance for weakness, sometimes I have to bite my tongue to prevent telling my friend when she is sounding like an ass.

"Get a dog," I suggest facetiously, applying humor to the absurdity of her ongoing dramatics.

"What?"

"Did you not hear me? I said, buy a dog."

My flippant remark does not register with her at first, but then I see Catherine's eyes transform into two half-moons. Her face creases, and the mirth she has kept suppressed for far too long bubbles up from somewhere deep inside her.

"Buy a dog!" she brays, and I join her laughter until both of us are clutching our sides and the tears are streaming from our eyes faster than we can wipe them away.

"Oh, how I will miss you!" she cries, plucking several facial tissues from a decorative box on my bureau and dabbing her eyes. She passes the box to me.

"You do realize I will only be gone three days, don't you?" I ask her, wiping my own eyes.

"Yes, of course. But three days without you, Frances, is an eternity for me." Her declaration quickens my heart.

I twist around to one of the dresses folded behind me on the bed and lift the selected piece of jewelry from its pleated bodice. Catherine chose it, not knowing it happens to be my most treasured piece. It is a solid gold locket with an etched cover that bears my mother's initials, *MWP.* It hangs from a length of fine gold roping and was my father's first gift to my mother over sixty years ago.

"Take it," I offer, dangling the locket by its chain and delicately dropping it into my friend's hand then folding her fingers over it before she can protest.

"Oh, I couldn't possibly!" Catherine gasps, overwhelmed by my generosity.

"I insist. I want you to have it. Consider it a little something to remember me by."

"Please don't say that. I really hate when you speak of death and dying. My emotions are way too fragile today without one of your maudlin reflections. It's morbid."

"Is that how I sound to you—morbid?"

"Yes. You speak as though you won't be coming back. It's only three days, after all."

"Oh, I'll be back all right, don't you worry about me." I rise up from the bed, albeit slowly. "Actually, I had been waiting for the right moment to give this locket to you and the moment has presented itself. Please accept it in appreciation for the tender care you provided me during my convalescence and for our many years together as devoted friends."

Fresh tears spring up in her eyes. Indeed, Catherine is more sensitive today than usual. Perhaps her emotions are what enable her to speak so candidly, for she takes me completely off guard when she says:—

140

"I am sorry, Frances, for never loving you the way you wanted or needed."

Catherine's words hang motionless in air for a spell, but eventually I find my voice.

"You have loved me well enough, though I admit to loving you more than is right for one woman to love another."

It is a declaration I was not prepared to make, and once again I am left feeling drained. It is imperative the subject be changed immediately.

"Kindly pass me my crutches, will you?" I ask. "I need you to do me a favor, if you don't mind."

I watch my friend, my love, loop the gold chain over her head and drop the locket under her blouse where I envision it resting against her heart. The gesture somewhat pacifies me, and I take my crutches from her and secure the cuffs to my forearms.

"I forgot to have Mary do this when she was here today," I begin, moving toward the one closet that had formerly housed my husband's wardrobe but which is now used for my own fashion excess. I point with my finger. "On the top shelf are my hatboxes. Take down the biggest one, if you can reach it."

Catherine enters the closet and stands on tiptoe, reaching high for the box, leaving me with a view of her most attractive derrière.

"What's in it?" she asks, backing out with the cumbersome box in her arms and setting it down on the boudoir chair.

"If I've guessed the right box, it should contain an enormous black straw hat, with a black satin band and a silk yellow rose stitched on one side."

Catherine slides the satin cord and lifts the lid of the box. She spreads apart the protective sheets of tissue and exposes the chapeau. "Oh! Frances, how utterly fashionable! May I try it on?"

"Of course you may. In fact, you may borrow it any time you wish."

"Oh! If only I had an occasion to wear something as fine and as stylish as this!"

I watch as first she drapes my silk shawl about her shoulders and then cocks her head to one side and positions the hat. She tilts her neck back to exhibit a face aglow with naturalness. The easy manner in which she adapts to simplicity or extravagance is a quality I highly admire in her. She performs a little pirouette for me.

"How do I look?"

"Very Bette Davis," I tell her, admiring the hat on Catherine's head far more than I ever did on my own. "That hat is one of my all-time summer favorites. I think I should wear it to the fundraiser, don't you?"

Catherine

Jack's ship arrives in port this afternoon, but he might as well already be sitting right here right now at our breakfast table, so present is he on each of our minds.

I gaze out the kitchen window and wonder if today's weather is a good omen. The morning dawned clearer than it has in weeks, but the air is also more heavy and humid than it has been. Weather-wise, this certainly has not been one of our typical Septembers.

The Wild Columbine, and the Sweet Pepperbush plants with their fiery harvest colors, all have bloomed either minimally this year or not at all.

This week, the sea has been rough and challenging, which has only served to cut short the vacations for tourists, many of whom enjoy occupying our beaches during this particular time of year. We have seen them packing their belongings into their vehicles before locking up their mildewed cottages and driving back to their prospective homes in neighboring states. Only the most resilient optimists lag behind, believing the weather here will soon improve. Eventually, it has to.

Soon after Lizzie left for school this morning the wind began to move in. Gradually it has picked up until now it is whipping the laundry on the clothes-line as though to punish the fabrics into drying. However, the humidity level is preventing them to dry quickly. I glance out the window every few minutes to make sure half of what I hung hasn't blown over onto our neighbor's yard.

My mind is completely on Jack and his arrival from Panama. No captain, no matter how experienced, can help but curse such a persistent bluster as what I can see happening outside. I imagine Jack and his crew on board and trust they have their wits are about them as they sail against the swells of an uneven tide.

Jonah hasn't touched the cheese and tomato sandwich I have put in front of him, but I see that he has chosen his best white shirt and flannel trousers to wear to his meeting with Jack. I also notice he has taken the time to polish his shoes, which assures me that some of the social graces I have tried to instill in him have apparently taken hold. Still, it is plain to see that my son is as jumpy as a bag of cats. He speaks little and slouches at the table while he nibbles at his cuticles and pumps his knee up and down until I gently press my hand upon it to make him stop.

William has done little but pace between the kitchen and his study. His face has been resolutely etched with a perpetual scowl of disapproval for two days now, and I notice he keeps pulling the timepiece from his vest pocket to refer to it. Between his body language and that of our son, I cannot tell if they wish time would move faster or stop entirely. Finally William chooses to speak, addressing Jonah:—

"I thought we would ride into town to gas the car. You can drop me off at the church on your way out."

Jonah stands up from the table and stretches. He pushes his luncheon plate with the uneaten sandwich gently toward me, an apology already on his lips.

"I'm sorry, but I'm just not hungry," he says.

He leaves the room, and already I can feel the lonely stab of separation, which all too soon will become a permanent loss when the Navy swears him in and claims him for its own. If it were within my power to do so, I would muster a brave front for Jonah's sake, but a cold blade stabs at my heart and leaves me to bleed with the anticipated loss of my firstborn. This has been the prevailing mood of late; and if it were not for Lizzie's larking about, our home would seem as solemn and somber as a Sunday service.

"What do you plan to do with yourself while we're gone?" William asks, interrupting my musings. "Have you errands to keep you occupied?"

"Why am I asked to account for this day when you have never asked me on any other day?" I volley. "I can't very well follow Jonah without a car, if that is your concern."

144

"The thought never crossed my mind. I was merely making conversation."

"Why now," I ask him, "when we have barely spoken more than a few sentences to each other for days?"

William, realizing he has opened a hornet's nest with me, groans and rubs his temples. "I will leave you then to do whatever it is ladies do on a day such as this."

"Perhaps get my hair done, or buy myself a new dress!" I quip, wiping my perspiring brow and wishing Frances was at home rather than in the Hamptons.

"Considering how fetching you are when you're mad," William winks, "I should say I am glad for this little exchange."

"And I suppose I will spend this day as I do most every other; that is, doing laundry, food shopping, and helping our daughter with her homework when she gets home."

The phone rings, and I get up to answer it. Elizabeth's school is releasing the children early, and the principal is requiring that the parents come for them. Jonah grumbles at first when he is asked to go, quickly realizes he must earn the privilege to take the car this afternoon.

I watch him walk off in the direction of the school, his hands shoved deep into his pockets, all the while pushing solidly against the wind. A loud crash sends me hurrying back through the kitchen and out to the porch, where William is already surveying the damage.

"Be damned, will you look at that?" he exclaims, scratching his head and looking up to the sky.

It is a shock to find the weighty wooden window box, which had been filled with the last of the season's marigolds, blown off the porch railing by the strong wind. It lay broken in four pieces upon the walk, with an array of stubby gold blossoms, their sprouted root systems protruding from solid chunks of dark soil, utterly strewn across the walk.

I tell William about the call from the school, glancing upward to read the sky. William goes inside to check the barometer and comes back out to report a reading of 29.90. Both of us know such a reading is by no means cause for alarm; but as coastline residents, we know how rapidly a shift in pressure can come about.

The wind playing havoc has William running down the porch steps in hot pursuit of our laundry basket, now seen tumbling across the yard to our neighbor's lawn. I am quick to follow as I head for the clothesline to snatch what is miraculously still hanging. Several pieces of laundry have been plucked from the line by the wind and are holding fast against the garden arbor. I free them, but another powerful gust all but wrestles the bag of clothespins from my hand. Clutching everything to my chest, I butt my head to the wind and follow on William's heels, back inside the house, with the screen door slamming right behind us.

"I've got to go back out and sweep up that mess," he says, heading once again for the blustery outdoors.

"Save what plants you can," I instruct him. "There's an empty pot in the garage. Just put them in that with some soil. I can replant them tomorrow."

I hear Jonah and Lizzie coming in through the front door. They enter the kitchen breathlessly, their hair this way and that.

"Whew! It could flip your wig out there!" Jonah exclaims, running his hands through his own mop of wavy hair.

"It was so hard to walk!" Lizzie chimes in. "Jonah had to walk behind me and push me a lot of the way!"

She comes to me when I motion to her, then fidgets while I try to smooth her hair and refasten her barrettes. "Mama, please sto-o-p!" she insists, pushing my hand away. "You treat me like I'm five years old!"

"I'm done," I say, quickly capturing a last abandoned curl. "There. Now, tell me what your teacher told the class before she let everyone go."

"She said if we have to stay indoors, we should do what our parents tell us and not to be afraid if the weather turns bad. I want to call Margaret to see if she got home yet," Lizzie announces, disappearing as quickly as an afterthought.

Jonah, who had gone upstairs, now comes back down carrying the camera Frances gave him for Christmas, along with his trumpet. I think he senses my apprehension, for he stands braced and ready to argue the point should I tell him he cannot take the car by himself. He smells faintly of smoke. I can see the red circle symbol of cigarettes faintly outlined through the pocket of his shirt but say nothing. Elizabeth had already tattled on him about sharing a smoke with his father when I was away. It only served to remind me that my son is no longer a boy to be easily directed.

We hear the velocity of the wind outside and I teeter on the brink of indecision. "Jonah, I am not sure you should drive alone."

"Don't be so hardboiled, Mother—it's just a little wind, that's all."

"Watch your tone, young man," I tell him, sternly. "I'm not at all sure about this weather; I want to hear what your father says when he comes in."

"But it's not raining, and the boats will be coming in as scheduled—I'm sure of it. I'll drive carefully, I promise, but if you are going to act squirrely about it, Father definitely isn't going let me take the car."

"What won't I do?" William asks, coming in and heading straight for the sink to wash his hands.

"I want to take the car by myself as we agreed, but Mother thinks I'm not a good enough driver."

"That's not true," I say. "I'm just worried about the wind." I implore William with a private look. "I don't want the car, with our son inside of it, being blown off the road."

"I'll go with him," William states flatly. He eyes the camera and trumpet case in his son's hands. "What do you plan to do with those?"

"I thought you might take a picture of me and Captain Wakefield." He gives the trumpet case a little shake. "And since I'm aces at playing marching songs, I want to play *Stars and Stripes Forever* as the boat docks."

"You will do nothing of the sort," William commands. "Leave them both at home. You will make a fine enough impression without either. Now say goodbye to your mother and Lizzie and let's get ready to go. Hurry up before I change my mind and we stay home."

Deflated, Jonah sets his belongings on the counter. He sees my own disappointment and mistakes it for concern, when in truth I am upset to know there now will be no photo of Jack for a keepsake.

"Goodbye, Mother," Jonah says, grazing my cheek with a quick peck. My face is frozen with resentment at William's going instead of me.

"Relax, Mother," Jonah says, "we will be fine." He tells me this, all the while a menacing wind whistles eerily outdoors as if to challenge his courage. I look Jonah in the eyes, but all I can see is Jack standing before me the last time I saw him...

It is 1921. We're standing on the dock at Cape Canal, where I have seen him leave from once before, only this time he won't be coming back. A strapping crew of sailors, both young and old, many being shipmates of Jack's, catcall to us from and cast knowing glances our way as they load supplies onto the deck of the merchant vessel they'll be boarding, bound for the Carolinas.

"How can you leave me, Jack?" I whimper, following a long tirade. "I am having your baby!"

147

Up until now, I have been pathetic in my begging, but now I twist his shirt in my clenched fists, as if I might wring his forgotten decency from the very fabric. I can feel my eyes wild with fear, so panicked am I that he has already made up his mind; and that no antics of mine, no matter how heartfelt, will convince him to stay. Afraid I have already lost the cause, my hands fall limply to my sides.

"There are things about me you don't know, Cat, things you would not understand. Believe me, I have no choice."

"We all have choices, Jack. For one, you could take me with you," I offer, knowing full well the impossibility of my solution. Even I can't imagine a life at sea with an expectant woman on board.

A crooked half-smile marks Jack's face. It is the first light moment between us in this desperate conversation. "You know that's not possible."

Jack pauses, taking my hands between his own. "You should accept Will's proposal." His voice, hoarse with emotion, already sounds far away to me. "He has loved you all along," he says. "There is no one truer—no other man who would be more devoted to you than Will. He will make a far better husband and father than I could ever be."

I play my last card. "If my father was still alive, you know that he would hold you accountable for my condition! Does it not bother you at all that you taint his memory by deserting me?"

"Not even your father, who you know I admired very much, could stop me from boarding this vessel today. I've told you I have to go and that you must stay. Will has promised me he will raise the child properly. Please, Cat, don't make this harder for me than it is. If you can't do it for me, do it for our baby."

"Don't make it hard for you?" An agonizing cry escapes my lips as I realize he will not be swayed.

I collapse, defeated, against his chest. "I thought it was you who loved me! I would have thought that no one, not even Will, could love me more than you do."

"That's true!" he whispers hoarsely, burying his face in my hair. "I love you so much that it is near killing me to leave you!"

"Then don't go, for your leaving will surely kill me!"

"Cat," Jack murmurs, kissing away my tears, "we both know you are stronger than that."

My grief is such that I can barely remember his finally pulling out of my arms to board the ship. Was the word 'goodbye' even spoken by either of us? I cannot recall, and so I say it now—to Jonah. To Jack.

"Goodbye, my love," I tell him and kiss the generous brow that, at this given moment, could be father or son. For me, they are one and the same.

Jonah walks away in search of his sister and William steps forward and rounds his finger under my chin that we might kiss, but I tilt my head away, refusing to meet his eyes. Perhaps he can read my mind, for he says:—

"Don't begrudge me for going, Catherine. Surely you know this is not something I would choose to do if I didn't think it was necessary."

"How can I not feel resentful? You have known for months how much I want to accompany Jonah today. It is bad enough you forbid me to do something I've looked forward to for a year now, but then to take my place! I feel I am being punished."

"Not at all, but the weather gives me good reason for going in your stead."

As is often the case with him, my husband offers no explanation other than a gentle press upon my shoulder.

"Stay home where you belong," he says gently, "and let me have one less thing to worry about should the weather take a turn for the worse."

I watch from the kitchen door as they head to the car, Jonah holding fast to the basket of snacks I have packed in case they get held up. They are holding their felt fedoras pressed to their chests as they bend against an unusually blustering wind.   I realize my husband's concern for our safety here at home and lay an open hand up against the screen to offer a silent prayer for their own safekeeping.

They have not been gone an hour when the wind begins to strengthen and the sky turns a daunting yellow.

Jonah

We've recapped the Joe Louis versus Max Schmeling match and second-guessed Hitler's strategy to bait Britain, France, and Russia. We've even discussed Rachel's curriculum at Rhode Island State College and my intention to ask for her hand once the Navy has issued me a post. I keep the conversation going to stop Father from obsessing about the weather for the duration of the drive to Wings Neck.

The sky is menacing, I'll give him that, and we can only see little, if any, demarcation between it and the ocean. Although I am doing a rather keen job of driving our flathead, I can tell Father is fretting about Mother and Lizzie back home alone. Already a carpet of dense fog has begun rolling off the sea, hampering our visibility with a salty mist guaranteed to turn to rain. Any moment I suspect Father is going to insist we turn the car around and head back home.

The wind, which has followed us from home to the Socony filling station, is literally spinning the gas sign like a whirligig. While I fuel our car, a wiry man in filthy overalls looks out from under the hood of a car he is working on. He makes his way towards us—all the while wiping his hands on a greasy red cloth he had hanging out of a pocket.

The dollar I am holding is nearly snatched up by the wind, but the man with greasy hands is faster than that and claims it before the wind carries it off.

"You picked the wrong day to be on the road," the man calls out, shoving the dollar into one pocket and digging in the other to make change. I tell him to keep the coin and ask if he sells candy bars.

"That I do, but my selection is small: Snickers, Red Hots, and Bonomo's Turkish Taffy."

I signal my father that I'll just be a minute and follow the man into the station, the interior of which is not much cleaner than the owner. He takes out two small cardboard boxes from a cooler, removes their shabby lids, and offers me the sparse selection that appears to have been in there for some time.

"Electric's been out for an hour now. I shouldn't be let'n out what's left of the cold by open'n the cooler, but a sale's a sale."

Two fat, pesky flies circle our heads. One finally lands on a bar inside the box, and the man quickly shuts the lid on it.

"Guess now you've only got one box to choose out of," he says, giving me a near-toothless smile. He removes the closed box with the fly in it and puts it back under the counter.

I choose a vanilla taffy bar and smack it with the flat of my hand on the top of his counter. I unwrap it and pop a good size chunk in my mouth. It's so stale, I can barely chew it. I close the wrapper over the remains and slip it into my pocket.

I'm trying to work a piece of taffy from my tooth with my tongue when the man asks why Father and I are out when there's a storm on the way. I tell him that we are meeting a boat sailing in to Wings Neck.

"Wings Neck, you say? That's a well-kept secret here. Sailors come through to pick up and drop off instead of hav'n to use the commercial docks. Not everybody knows about that place— we like keep'n it to ourselves. Though if word were to leak out about it, I suppose business would increase for me; I could sure use that."

He extracts a squashed pack of smokes from his overalls and steadies a match to the tip of a sorry-looking butt.

"You can bet there'll be no boats sail'n in today—word is this weather's turn'n wicked bad. If I was you and your father out there, I'd get myself to someplace dry and stay there till the storm front has come and gone."

As if he heard his name mentioned, we hear a double honking of the car horn to mark my Father's impatience. I thank the man and bid him goodbye. Stepping back outside, I notice the wind has stopped.

"Looks like it's not going to be so bad after all," I comment.

Glancing up, I see not a single bird in the sky. In fact, the air is so close and unmoving, there is barely any to breathe.

"Don't let it fool you," the man cautions, squinting up at the darkening sky. "It's the calm before the storm. Be careful, son."

Father has his head sticking out the window. He looks hot and irritable. I take my place behind the wheel and offer him a piece of taffy, which he waves off. I know better than to mention the attendant's weather warning.

"The cheese sandwich your mother sent along would have been better for you than candy."

"It's been sitting too long; the tomato is soggy by now. Wait a minute." I reach back to the car floor and grab the bag with the sandwich in it. Spotting a nearby trash can, I step out of the car and deposit the sandwich in it.

"That's a waste of good food," Father says, adding, "but there's nothing worse than a warm tomato sandwich. Just don't let your mother know you did that."

The tires are trying to grip pavement as we make the final turn onto Wings Neck Road. They slip and slide through deep ribbons of damp sand that has been blown across the road by the wind. The car slithers like a snake, inching us toward the lighthouse as we watch for the parking lot we are certain lies beyond. That's where we plan to wait and watch for the first sign of Jack's fishing boat when it finally pierces the fog and shows itself.

"Keep your hands on the wheel, Jonah, and downshift to second," Father warns. "It looks like there's a tree limb down, just up ahead."

"I see it," I say, shifting too quickly. The gears grind unmercifully, setting our teeth to rattling with the bucking and jolting of it.

I bring the car to a stop just short of two sprawling oak limbs stretched across both lanes of the highway. Gnarly branches reach out like needy arms in the gray afternoon, shedding thousands of dried leaves to blow frantically about.

Judging from the size of the boughs, it will require two of us to move them. While assessing how to best accomplish this, the car's interior is suddenly bathed in a mustard-colored hue, and a chilling echo, like that of a woman screaming, can be heard far off in the distance. We look through the windshield to the sky above—it's a color not even my father has ever seen before.

The rain is beginning to pelt, but the howling of the wind is terrifying enough to make us regret having stepped out of the car. In a matter of seconds, our clothes are soaked through and already weighing us down.

Father shouts an order, but the wind is whistling too loudly for me to hear his words. He makes a motion with his hands and grabs the heaviest end of one bough. I move to the opposite end and together we half-lift, half-drag the heavy limbs to the side of the road, enough to give us passage with our car. The sky opens, and we make a beeline for the car, with Father sliding in behind the wheel. Rain beats angrily upon the roof of the car; water is forming in shallow pools in the leather seats and at our feet.

"Damnation! The man's not worth this!" Father curses under his breath. He squeezes his mouth roughly with one hand, glaring defiantly at a windshield we can't see out of. "Just look at it out there!" he says, pointing with his finger. "It's impossible to see your hand in front of your face! No man in his right mind would choose to sail in this. If I know Jack, he knew about the forecast and never even left port! We have ventured out for nothing!"

My disappointment surprises even myself. "I hope not," I admit. "Do you really think he would have stayed in port and not sent word?"

"Sure he would! He's a master at using people and then letting them down!" Father accuses.

It's rare to see my father this worked up, but I know enough not to fan his anger by commenting any further. I keep my eyes fixed on the torrential rain, which shows no sign of subsiding any time soon.

Like steam escaping through a pipe, Father exhales loudly and rolls his head backward to rest on the seat while he closes his eyes against the beating of the rain. Only then do I dare to look over at him. His face is as unmoving as a mask, and I remain still and uncomfortable until he opens his eyes a few moments later and catches me staring at him.

"I'm sorry," Father apologizes. He starts the engine. "I had no right to say that, especially when it's not true."

A gust of wind rocks the car, and I shiver——in part because I'm chilled, but partly because I'm fearful Jack won't come.

"What's not true?" I ask.

"That Jack was a master at disappointing people. I am sure there are many who would disagree with that remark."

"He disappointed Mother," I point out.

"That he did," Father agrees. "But obviously, his loss was my gain, now wasn't it?"

Father is operating the car at a crawl, staring ahead as if he can see a fraction of the past hovering up ahead on the road.

I envision myself in the Navy and someday with Rachel and hope that one day I might experience the best of both worlds: adventure at sea *and* marrying the girl I love. I ask Father:—

"You don't hate him for it?"

"You mean Jack? No, son, I don't hate him. I couldn't hate Jack, though he has given me reason to. You would have to know him as long and as well as I did to understand why I say that."

"There are so many missing pieces to the story of Jack Wakefield. I'm confused how I feel about him," I admit.

Barely able to see across the road, we can just make out waves breaking against the boulders that form the rock jetty. We're traveling at a snail's pace.

"Ever since he was a boy, Jack pushed the limits. He got away with doing and saying things no one else could. Being a preacher's son, I lived vicariously through Jack, who wasn't afraid to try anything. He was daring; he took chances—risky ones that only crazy people would dare to try. And maybe he himself was crazy. He had the devil in him, that's for sure, but anyone who knew Jack would say that was just another part of his appeal."

"I didn't think you tolerate the devil in anyone, Father," I say, resentful that he will make an excuse for his friend's shortcomings when he is always so fast to point a finger at mine.

"People used to refer to Jack as *The Golden Child*," Father says loudly, raising his voice to be heard. "When you finally meet him, you'll see exactly what I mean.

We say no more, for a banshee wind has suddenly reared its ugly head. It comes barreling and screaming across an angry sea, bearing down on Cape Cod like a runaway train.

Frances

"Quick! Carry her to the house!" Harriet Sims shouts above the wind into the ear of a tall man standing beside us.

We all are at this magnificent fundraiser, where I toasted what I mistakenly presumed to be a bit of inclement weather. The next moment, the skies opened, and I am being carried off, highball in hand, in the arms of a total stranger.

Whoever he is, he's as agile as a quarterback. He sidesteps the pandemonium, making his way to the main house, where the lighted windows beckon us to shelter.

Harriet demands a small chaise, where I am deposited heavily upon its tufted cushions and left in her overwrought care. My hero is gone before I have the chance to thank him, and I make a mental note to find him once the storm passes.

My crutches have been left outside, forgotten in the chaos of a storm that has battered the island at lightning speed, causing those of us who were outdoors to scatter like ants whose nest has been invaded. When I ask Harriet if someone can go fetch them for me, she looks at me as if I have lost my mind.

Inside this grand old homestead, all but the injured are moving about. Everyone is talking at once, each person trying to assess the storm, with no one absolutely sure of its potential severity. The women are dazed and disheveled, wringing their hands and carrying on about their ruined garments. Every man is equally uncomfortable in his wet clothing, but rather than complain, they sensibly do what they can to secure the windows and shutters.

"The phone's not working! I can't reach the operator," exclaims an austere woman, who earlier had thought to impress me with her social affiliations. She panics, frantically tapping the cradle of a black phone to no avail.

Several lamps in the room flicker repeatedly before finally going out. Instantly, the room goes silent as each of us realizes that in less than an hour we will be submerged in total darkness.

A housemaid leaves the room and returns a few minutes later with a candelabra and a box of wooden matches. She sets the ornate fixture atop the ledge of the ebony grand piano and lights six wax tapers. The candles cast a pinkish glow, illuminating the perspiring faces of those gathered around.

This handsome old manor house, staunch and unyielding, shudders and moans, its creaking joints protesting against the sudden forces that seem hellbent on demolishing it. Through the walls we can hear the frightened voices of other occupants scrambling about in search of candles, all the while the poltergeist outside showing no sign of relenting.

I feel a familiar tightening in my chest. It comes upon me like an unwanted relative that one hopes never to see again. I pretend the passing discomfort is just my imagination, but I know exactly what it is, and I tremble at the telltale sign.

As we were taught to do when I was at the clinic, I practice a form of relaxation by closing my eyes and calling on an intimate memory...

"Dear God!" Catherine wails, her eyes bulging with the pain of labor, "how much longer? I am being ripped in two!"

"Soon, Catherine, soon," I reassure her, soothing her sweating brow with a cool cloth, while the doctor gloves his hands and parts Catherine's knees in readiness for the delivery.

My friend tries to raise herself up on her forearms but fails. "Where is Jack?" she cries. "I want Jack! Why isn't he here yet?"

Another contraction grips her womb, and her grimacing face contorts in pain. She pulls tightly on a long silk scarf I had removed from around my neck and tied to the bedpost.

I settle Catherine back upon the pillows. "You mean William. He had to make a sick call, don't you remember? The operator has rung him; he is on his way."

158

Catherine grasps my hand and crushes it fiercely. I have never seen her so deathly pale. She leans over and whispers to me in a voice rasping from pain:—

"You are here for me, aren't you, Frances? Jack is not here, nor is William; but you—you are always here for me."

"I always will be," I assure her.

Quickly the doctor motions to me that the baby is coming. I pull my hand from Catherine's and move to the foot of the bed just in time to see the pink, fuzzy skull of the baby's head as it crowns. Seconds later it makes its quick, slippery entrance into the world.

"It's a boy!" the doctor announces, swiftly cutting the cord between mother and child and holding the infant up for Catherine to see.

"Oh, Jack," Catherine cries, "isn't he beautiful?"

"He is very beautiful," I answer, ignoring her mistake.

The doctor cleans the baby, and I take Catherine's hand in mine. Our fingers intertwine, cosmically connecting us to the moment. And when the child is finally placed in her arms, one look has my friend totally and utterly in love with the tiny face gazing back at her.

"What shall we name him?" I ask, as if the child is our own.

"Jonah," Catherine says with conviction.

"Jonah," I repeat, hearing the name roll off my tongue. A little boy for us to love...

A thunderous crash quakes the very foundation of the estate, sending a Limoges vase toppling to the floor to shatter into smithereens. The stately grandfather clock in the corner of the living room teeters, its triple brass weights knocking together as they ring out a rippling of deafening dongs.

The woman standing nearest to Harriet and me flings her body into the protective arms of her husband, burying her face on his ample chest. "Lord, deliver us!" she cries, "The very walls are caving in!"

All at once we are assaulted by humidity, thick and oppressive, carrying with it the stench of low tide. It hangs heavily in the room, making it even more difficult to breathe. A lanky servant boy, whose white service uniform is a size too small for him, leaves the room to investigate. Minutes later he returns, visibly shaken. He tries to whisper his findings to one of the men but his words are overheard by those standing close by.

A stout patrician, with the complexion of a prune, is near to fainting from the news. She swoons against her equally corpulent husband, who slips a practiced hand discreetly into his jacket pocket and brings out a tiny vial of smelling salts. Quickly he uncaps the bottle and waves it twice under his wife's bulbous nose. The pungent sting of ammonia makes her whip back her head as she comes to, her embarrassment causing her face to crumble even more as she realizes she has been observed by everyone around her.

"Someone must go for help," a voice from behind suggests. "Send one of the lackeys!"

"Are you all right?" Harriet asks me, leaning close and placing a protective arm about my shoulders. "You are dreadfully ashen!"

"I-I'm just o-overly warm," I say, hearing the return of my former stammer reverberate in my ears.

"Christ in heaven! Will you look at that!" a man shouts, pointing out toward the sea. In seconds, everyone rushes to the window, pushing and straining to look out beyond the raging storm.

"What is it?" Harriet asks, unwilling to leave me to have a look herself.

"It's an entire *house!*" the man exclaims, his tragic expression dramatically veiled in candlelight. "It's a damned estate, completely blown out to sea! We're doomed!"

"It is *ours!*" one woman shrieks. "My God, Vincent, it's ours! " She collapses in a heap on the floor.

The nearly unrecognizable figure of Dr. Jeremy Sims comes unsteadily through the living room entryway. His wife, Davina bleeding from a head wound, is draped limply in his outstretched arms. "Make way! Please, let me pass!" he blurts out, staggering toward the stairway where Harriet and I are still crouched.

At the sight of them, my heart constricts again, this time sending a lightning bolt of pain to my chest and another to my head, like a double gunshot wound. I can feel the entire left side of my face slide in an avalanche of slackness.

I hear Harriet whimpering, first crying out her sister's name and then mine, though her voice sounds far away:—

"Frances! Frances, can you hear me? Jeremy, please!" I hear her beg him, "Frances needs your help!"

The blurred vision of the doctor's foot on the step moves the last of my remaining strength, and I slip my shaking hand through the banister spindles to clutch the fabric of his pant leg.

"I'll be back for you both!" Jeremy says, and I feel the cloth pulled from my fingers as he bounds up the stairs carrying his wife's limp form.

160

There is a shattering of glass and the sound of a woman screaming. *Or is it the wind?* It is becoming increasingly more difficult to breathe, and Harriet's mask of concern is growing dim before my eyes. I realize something serious is happening to me; but oddly enough, I am not afraid.

The sudden, woeful ripping of the ceiling boards splintering above is a terrifying sound. Immediately the pelting storm and the cold, salty spray of the sea rains down, drenching everything and everyone huddled below. Thunder, the likes of which I've never heard, crescendos above, and I rotate my head backward in time to witness a jagged bolt of lightning, its lethal voltage show-casing the insane asylum above. My heart constricts tighter yet as I fear hell's bottomless pit has risen and has been splayed open. There hovers a colossal living wall of tumultuous waters and tumbling sand, pulsating with a tonnage of shattered debris and living sea life, towering where only moments before a roof existed.

I watch with frozen horror as it crests mightily before beginning its tumbling, violently murderous descent. The sight is paralyzing; and at the very instant when I feel my terrorized heart cease to beat, my strangled voice shouts out Catherine's name like a battle cry.

Jonah

Rachel used to tell me about her adventures observing case-study hurricanes with her parents. When I asked her if she ever felt afraid, she said, "Only if my father was."

That's how I feel now, watching my father's trembling hands as he holds the steering wheel steady, trying to navigate our car to safety. Even with the accelerator pressed to the floor, our car is only able to move at a crawl against the resistance of the storm. We inch our way toward the beacon light, which we can see flashing intermittently in the distance on the lighthouse at Wings Neck. There is no way we can remain in this car and trust the keeper to offer us shelter—if we even make it that far.

The sea is disturbed and violent, rolling unceasingly as it thrusts angry waves toward shore. Each one explodes in a fury against the barricade of boulders that form the stone jetty to the left of us. With every eruption, our car is doused in churning seawater and the road becomes covered with foam. The water recedes and returns in even intervals, each assault seeming worse than the one before it.

It takes over an hour for us to cover one mile, but eventually the towering lighthouse that looked so small in the distance comes into full view.

Too late I realize how selfish it was of me to want to come today, especially when my mother's intuition advised against it. I know now that no sailor in his right mind would choose to sail this raging sea, and I fear for any who may have tried.

The fog is dense, but not so thick that we miss two beaming headlights lighting a tiny alcove just ahead of us. We can tell by their positioning that the automobile is turned on its side.

As Father inches our car closer, the vehicle resembles a seafaring gray ghost, with most of its color having been sandblasted off by the battering of sand and storm. Its front bumper is gone and the driver's door has been torn from its hinges. The passenger door is completely inaccessible, trapped against the boulders that form the rock jetty.

"I'll check it out and see if anyone's in there," I volunteer, leaning my weight against the car door to open it. But Father has already exited the car and is crossing the road.

"There's a couple inside!" Father screams to me above the squall.

I peer into the cab. A fellow about my age is slumped across a female whose youthful bare limbs are poking out awkwardly underneath him. I steady my stance and brace myself to receive the guy as Father pulls him from the interior and passes him into my waiting arms. There is a sizable gash in the fellow's forearm, but the rain is rinsing the wound faster than it can bleed. He has no inkling where he is, so I wrap his good arm securely around my neck and instruct him to lean on me.

"What's your name?" I shout. He mutters a name, but I can't hear him. I try again. "Who are you?"

"Frank!" he says louder, "Frank...Harrington!"

I'm walking him in a circle to help keep Frank coherent, but the wind is fighting us every inch of the way.

"Put him in our car!" Father yells. He is bent over the cab again, trying his best to get a grip on the other passenger.

I turn with my arm around Frank, but our car is not there— at least not where it was. *What the hell?*

Straining beneath Frank's weight, I look around in the blinding rain and spot the car nearly a quarter mile down the road. It's hydroplaning—twirling freely in the dirty churning water. We watch, stupefied, until the vehicle's route is finally blocked by a pile of wooded debris.

Father pulls back, half-dragging an unconscious female from the passenger seat. She is drooping like a drowned rat, but I can tell by her shapely, skimpily-dressed figure she's a *babe*. Father hoists her over his shoulder as easily as if she's a sack of potatoes; her dark is hanging like wet snakes, her pretty arms dangling lifelessly behind his back.

Father turns his back to us; I am rewarded—despite the blinding rain—with a clear view of the girl's fleshy bottom, showing clearly through the soaked fabric of her cotton dress and her (now transparent) underwear, and I react with the typical stirrings of a full-blooded male.

"Where the hell's our car?" Father thunders, slipping and sliding in the wet sand.

I point my finger in the direction of the road, and he curses loudly.

"Let's head for the lighthouse!" I shout. "It's closer!"

We make our way in the dark, gripped in the stronghold of the storm and a foot of swirling water above our ankles, fearful that the angry sea might rise any minute and burst through the barricade of rock wall.

We keep our eyes focused on the keeper's house up ahead, with its candle-lit window and promise of safety. Hopefully the owner will give us a change of clothes and some food and let us stay till whatever this is blows over.

We finally cross the sparse lawn to the house and stumble up the stone steps of the house. There's a brass plate on the door that reads:

Clarance P. Donnerman
Lighthouse Keeper, Wings Neck

Bypassing the tiny brass knocker, I bang my fist loudly upon the heavy wood door. Seconds feel like hours, but finally a burly man with a mustache and a look of surprise opens the door a crack to peer at us through candlelight.

"Please, Mr. Donnerman, we need your help," Father yells, above a gust of wind that forces the door open wider and all but ushers us over the threshold.

"Hurry in!" Mr. Donnerman shouts, pulling us out of the way, then pressing his full weight against the door and throwing the bolt to secure it.

The house, though damp, is as still as a tomb compared to what we've just come in from, and I near but faint for how good it feels at this very moment.

Pointing to the girl, Mr. Donnerman asks, "Is she all right? There's a couch in there," he says, directing us to the tiny room ahead.

He leads us in, viewing us as if we're a fisherman's bad catch. The moisture inside this place is so tangible and thick, it penetrates my sinuses. Still, I'm grateful for shelter.

"I am Reverend McFarley, and this is my son, Jonah," Father says, winded, gently lowering the girl from his shoulder and propping her up against the couch, where she remains with her head down and her chin on her chest.

"Our car has floated some ways off; and this unfortunate pair had theirs overturn a short way from here. Can we stay with you until the lines are up and we are able to call for help?"

"Of course—you must," Mr. Donnerman says, already crossing to a side table to pour a shot of brandy in a glass tumbler. "Give the girl a sip of this—it'll restore her color."

Mr. Donnerman holds the candle above my father's head as he sits beside the girl and offers the tumbler to her bluish lips. She lifts her face and wipes her hair out of her face to take a sip, and now I can clearly see her in the glow of candlelight.

My mouth opens in total disbelief, for the girl lying helplessly in my father's supportive arms is none other than Alice Brighton!

Frank is hovering at the window. "Look!" he calls out, pointing to the dark of night. "See out there! It's a ship's light!"

I rush to the window and immediately feel the steady placement of my father's hand on my shoulder. We see the speck of light, which disappears every few seconds and reappears like an *S.O.S.* message for help.

Mr. Donnerman, whose face is grave with concern, verifies that it a vessel being tossed about in the troughs, struggling to stay afloat. His trained eye scans the waters for help.

I turn to Father. "Do you think it's him?"

"I would not be surprised," he says, keeping his eye on the light.

I bolt from the room and am down the steps in a matter of seconds—running across the yard, stumbling and tripping in the deep, saturated sand of the beach, screaming all the way. Waves are pounding the jetty rocks, bursting in enormous sprays that lather me in foam and shredded seaweed, and all I can taste is salt.

"JACK! JAA-C-K!" I shriek, long and loud, cupping my hands around my mouth.

I wave my arms frantically in a crisscross pattern above my head, hoping someone on the boat will spot me beneath the repetitive passing of the lighthouse beam as it moves across the up-churned waters, but I am in the shadowed light far below it. Behind me, I can hear Father screaming out my name. I turn to see him trying to make his way through the curtain of swirling rain. There is no time to spare.

I turn my head back to the sea, the full force of the gale in my face. My squinting eyes scan the perimeter of inky sea until I spot what I believe to be Jack's boat, with its tiny glimmer of light. *Is it my imagination or has the light diminished in size?*

Panting, Father stumbles to my side, gripping me by the arm. "Jonah, come back inside! They can't hear you!"

"It's Jack's boat!" I scream, "I just know it is!"

We watch the light, with our arms around each other and the rain in our eyes. It flickers as the boat is tossed about like a toy, and then suddenly, the light goes out.

We wait, in silence, the rain beating its endless tempo of doom. My heart is pounding, but we continue to wait for what seems a lifetime, watching for a light that does not reappear.

Fearing the worst, I drop to my knees. My eyes are glued to the spot where I think we saw the flickering brightness; and when minutes go by and nothing happens, I believe I feel my heart break with despair, and I wish only for the ground to open up to swallow me whole.

"Please, son, let's go back inside!" Father begs.

"Leave me!" I wail loudly, folding in misery.

But my father does not let me go, and I hear his words spoken forcefully and closely in my ear:—

"I will *never* leave you!" he screams out.

I cover my face with both hands, bending even further into myself, and feel the pounding of the rain, beating on my back like a punishment.

Catherine

Elizabeth is on the brink of hysteria, probably reacting to my own tension and what the radio announcer is terming a *tropical cyclone*.

I am sick with worry for my husband and son, who have been gone for five hours now. My prayer is for them—and of course for Jack, who I pray had enough foresight to predict the weather and stay on land.

Adding to my worries is my concern for Frances. Edward phoned an hour ago to say that Westhampton had been hard hit and that he has been unable to get in touch with his aunt. He promised to let me know as soon as he's had word from her, but our phone lines went down shortly thereafter. If he has been trying to reach me, he cannot get through.

Our street looks like a ghost town, which is why I am alarmed when I see Benjamin Fromlehide pull up in front of our house in his hearse. He emerges from the ominous carrier under the protection of an enormous black umbrella, which is immediately turned inside out, rendering it completely useless. As he hurries up the path to our porch, I can see he is dressed in his habitual sombre attire and that his face is set with such a sullen expression, I am almost afraid to open the door.

Elizabeth, already on the edge, her eyes wide as saucers, asks:—

"Does he have a dead body in his car?"

169

"He has probably come to see your father," I say reassuringly, moving her off to one side and opening the door just enough to let in our guest.

"Catherine, I am sorry to intrude!" the undertaker says, his clothes plastered to his bony frame as he brings the deluge in with him.

"Benjamin, I cannot believe you are driving in this!" I say, pulling him all the way in and quickly and closing the door. He reaches out to pat Elizabeth on the head, but she recoils.

"I see you are still shy," he says to her, leaning over the knob of his cane and extending his neck like a vulture so that his face is level with hers. "There is no need to be—I like children."

"Catherine, forgive the intrusion," he says, standing up. "I would not have come out in this were it not important. I must speak to William—Jonah, too, if you don't mind."

"I'm afraid you've come for naught, Benjamin. William and Jonah are not here," I tell him. "Like you, they are out driving in this, though who knew the day would take such an awful turn?"

Benjamin is shocked. "Where did they go? Surely not far! Please tell me they are expected soon."

"If only that was the case. They left hours ago to meet a boat at Wings Neck. We are...um...expecting a guest."

He gives a sideways glance at Elizabeth, who is still riveted at my side. "May we speak privately for a moment?" he asks me.

"Of course," I say, extending a hand toward William's study and following behind him. Lizzie tries to come with us, but I stop her at the door and tell her she is to wait in the hall. She gives me a fearful look as I join close the door on her.

"Your business with William must be important to bring you out in this," I say, pointing Benjamin toward a chair.

"I have just received a frantic call from Doris Brighton. She tells me Alice is missing."

"Perhaps she is at a friend's house and cannot call home. The phones are out, as you well know."

"Apparently, she left to go for a drive with a young man who is sweet on her," He explains. "They left this morning before the weather changed. Doris says she insisted Alice be home by noon. It is now five o'clock. She has not been heard from all day."

"How can we be of help?" I ask.

"I thought perhaps Jonah might be able to shed some light on her where-abouts."

"Why would Jonah know where she is?" I ask, somewhat confused.

Benjamin shifts his cane from one hand to the other. "It's just a shot in the dark, but I thought Jonah—being a young man and all—-that he might know.

"Know what?" I bristle, beginning to feel unnerved.

"This is rather delicate. I know Jonah and Rachel Coulter were seeing each other while she and her family were living on Cape..." His voice trails off.

"I don't understand. What does my son's relationship with Rachel have to do with Alice Brighton?"

"I thought Jonah would probably know where...where the young people go to make *whoopee*," he blurts out, clearly uncomfortable with the subject.

My mouth falls open at the mere insinuation that Jonah and Rachel do this, though there is some speculation in my mind that they have. "Wouldn't the police be more likely to be of help?

"Of course, but Mrs. Brighton was hoping it wouldn't have to come to that. When she called on me this afternoon neither of us had any premonition the weather would take such a serious turn. I'm sure you can understand that she was hoping to keep Alice's escapade a private matter. It was my sugges-tion that perhaps Jonah, being of Alice's age, might know of some... *hide-aways*. We have checked the usual spots—the movie theatre, soda shops, and such. I realize we are grabbing at straws here." He removes a handker-chief from his pocket and dabs at his brow. "Oh, my—this is a most uncom-fortable matter."

An already raging wind does the answering for me. It turns insane out-side, encompassing the house like a witch on her broom, screaming its de-structive terror. Alice Brighton is immediately forgotten as I remember my daughter standing alone in the hall. When I open the study door, Lizzie flies into my arms.

"Mama, I'm really scared! Where are Father and Jonah? How do we know they are safe?" she cries.

"Shush, Lizzie, you must trust that they are. Remember, your father grew up here. He knows the Cape inside and out. He and your brother are prob-ably in a cozy sandwich shop right about now."

Lizzie looks at me, searching for the slightest sign of uncertainty on my face.

"Besides," I add, "God is watching over them and keeping them safe."

As if to disagree, the wind is shrieking its fury. It shakes our sturdy house to its very foundation as it takes out all the electrical lines at the same time, leaving the entire street in the near dark of late afternoon.

"I must get the candles," I announce. I loosen my daughter's grip on me, but she follows behind me like a puppy afraid to be left alone. Benjamin joins us in the parlor.

I open the drawer of an antique highboy William and I inherited from his parents when we were first married. It smells as ancient and familiar as it is to me. As I feel for the candles in the back of the drawer, I am suddenly overcome by an overwhelming desire to be reunited with my husband, our son, and my dear friend, Frances.

Rachel and her family also spring to mind. *Is Rhode Island faring all right?* Alice Brighton's whereabouts has me concerned, too. Her mother must be as frantic as I, wondering whether or not those we love are safe. Emotional uncertainty suddenly rushes up from the depths of my heart, and I burst into tears.

My daughter wraps her arms around me, and Benjamin encircles us with a bony hand upon our shoulders. To my surprise, Lizzie does not move away this time. Instead we stand triangular, united in friendship and overall concern.

"Your rugged men will return safely," he assures us, "and Alice Brighton and the boy will be found."

"Frances Gellermont is away from home, as well," I say, composing myself and lighting the tapers. I place them where they will shed the most light. "She is in Westhampton for the weekend."

"I suspect she is fine," Benjamin assuages. "This is probably an isolated nor'easter on Cape. For all you know, Frances could be enjoying sunny skies on Long Island."

"Won't you stay and share a bit of dinner with us?" I ask, suddenly grateful for his optimistic outlook.

"Thank you. It isn't often I have the pleasure of sharing a meal. Besides, I must stay until this wretched weather subsides."

Back in the kitchen, I pull out a plate of cold chicken, a generous wedge of Swiss cheese, a bowl of leftover cucumber salad with sliced red onion, and a pitcher of cool tea. Lizzie opens the breadbox and takes out a half loaf of bread. We put everything on the table, along with condiments, plus a small vase of mint sprigs for our tea.

Over the meager fare, Benjamin keeps our minds occupied with his retelling of tales and half-truths about the great nor'easters he has survived in his lifetime, none of which are making Lizzie or myself feel any safer. I can tell by the way his brow is etched with concern that none of the storms he is describing were as severe as what we are experiencing right now.

Whether or not he hexed himself by reliving the atmospheric accounts of his past, our meal is suddenly interrupted by a crash outside with the resonance of shattering glass.

The three of us rush from the table to look out the living room window. It is necessary to squint in order to see beyond the heavy downpour, but the damage is obvious. A set of house shutters have been shot airborne by the raging wind and have completely shattered the windshield of the undertaker's Packard hearse.

Benjamin Fromlehide goes into a tirade! He rants and curses under his breath, banging his cane so heavily upon the floor that I must insist he regain his composure. Still, he cannot keep from pacing the floor of the stuffy parlor, glancing out the window and carrying on each time he looks upon the tragic scene.

The street is flooded; and the hearse, still elegant despite its damaging blow, is a classic amongst the ruins. Broken fencing, a rowboat adrift, bicycles, deck chairs, rafters, and fallen shrubbery—phantom objects all—in a graveyard of disaster.

With little choice, Benjamin has settled down while Lizzie and I return to the kitchen to clear the table of food that is no longer wanted. We go from room to room, rolling dish towels lengthwise and pressing them against the seams of every window sill, both upstairs and down. Next, we do the same with two bath towels, securing one at the base of both the front door and the one in the kitchen. While this is a suitable remedy for preventing the rain from coming through, it has also served to make the house even more stifling than it already was.

To help Lizzie from feeling any more anxious, I suggest a mindless game of checkers. Mr. Fromlehide politely declines, preferring to watch the demolition of the storm.

I take out the large wooden checker board from the hall closet, along with a box of marble checkers, pointing out that we may be somewhat hampered by the lack of light. Lizzie chooses the red checkers, leaving me the amber ones. I pick one up and turn it over and over in my hand, feeling its cool, weighty smoothness. I've always loved these marble checkers, which belonged to my father—each shaped like a small patty that makes an interesting clicking noise when stacked atop another.

Elizabeth, intuitive enough to see I am not up to competing, takes full advantage, cringing from the sounds of the storm but managing to end the round with a calculated move, declaring herself winner.

All the while we've been playing I've been in silent misery, biting my cuticles and listening for the pounding rain to let up. Lizzie mistakes my melancholy for poor sportsmanship. She leans sideways in her seat and kisses my cheek, assuring me that if I try a little harder, I just may win the next round. Darling girl! I cannot resist her! But another round of checkers is not what I need, and I say so.

Lizzie gets up from her seat and stands before me. She wraps her arms lovingly around my neck. I seek comfort by burying my nose in the earthy fragrance of her hair and brush my brow against the petal softness of her rounded cheek. Her smell is comforting to me—so much so, I wish I could hide in it until William and Jonah return and our little family is whole again.

My lips travel to the noticeable freckle between her neck and shoulder, which I have referred to as her *kissing spot* since the day she was born. I blow a light raspberry there and hear her laugh. She squirms then, lifting her rounded shoulder to her cheek, and I pull away, swallowing the lump of worry that has been stuck in my throat since this hell began. Only innocent youth can find something to giggle about in an otherwise catastrophic nightmare.

My mind is a precipice of fear for the three men in my life. I wonder where they are at this moment, and I pray that, wherever they are, all three of them are under cover.

My worry over Frances is equally disturbing. *My dearest, truest of friend—of all the time for you to be gone!* The phone lines are still out of service. Therefore, I have no idea whether or not Edward has had any word from her.

Jack

Be damned if the people of Panama weren't right and I was wrong. They predicted that a storm front would spawn a cyclone off the coast of Africa and, by God, it has! Not only did the monstrosity hunt us down with a vengeance, but our second-hand fishing boat has been caught up in the mortal jaws of the bitch for the better part of ten hours.

Since the height of the storm, the three of us have pulled the weight of six men; and since I coerced them into joining me on this trip, my two buddies have every right to hold a grudge. Instead, they stand with me, their lives in danger, and place no blame nor complain any more than usual. I couldn't have asked for a better band of brothers.

Thomas Gunther and Vinnie 'Brando' Fuccelli: the three of us met in Alaska in '21, aboard the *SS Anchorage*—a ship of 140 crewmen, with every man packed into tight living quarters and working under strained and uncompromising conditions. We were among the few who didn't brawl like cellmates in a prison. We share political views and believe a man's handshake is as good as a signed contract. Over time, confined on the *Anchorage,* we developed a mutual respect, bonding to the point where we had each other's backs. It's been that way since we boarded the *Anchorage.* It's still the same now, aboard *Triton's Zodiac.* Nothing's changed.

Thomas is as black as ebony and as tall as a drink of water. He was born in Baton Rouge and is wise beyond his twenty-five years, plus he makes fish stew like nobody's business. His father was a shrimper, who beat his wife and son regularly. As Thomas tells it, he tried to offer his mother a better life when he was old enough. He begged her to join him in an escape plan, but she was already beaten down with self-loathing and declined his rescue, opting to remain behind. Though it pained Thomas to leave her, he chose the high road, running away one afternoon before his old man's boat had docked. With little more than a satchel of old clothes and some stolen food from the kitchen pantry, Thomas hopped a train bound for Washington. From there he sailed to Alaska and was hired by the trading company we now work for. The *SS Anchorage* became his new home and its crew, his new family. Thomas never looked back.

Vinnie 'Brando' Fuccelli is our rigger. He is a handsome, barrel-chested man, with a heart as broad as his shoulders. Vinnie keeps order on deck. He furls and releases *Zodiac's* nets, and when we stop in port to fuel, it's Vinnie's coercion that squeezes coin out of the tight-fisted merchants who want our fish without having to pay our asking price. Vinnie is also a novice astronomer. He reads the skies and the weather and, after applying his detections to our navigational board, gives me his opinion on the best course to take, whether I seek it or not. He is uneducated, only in that he never bothered to go to school.

Vinnie lived in the tenements of lower Manhattan, unofficially working as a laborer on the docks when he was only ten years old. He grew up and married an Italian shoemaker's daughter. They had a child together—a little girl. One day he came home to find both of them dead outside the apartment, victims of a gang fight. After their funeral, Vinnie sold what few belongings they had. He closed up the apartment and took a job as a riveter in the bowels of a steamer ship, eventually working his way to Alaska. But no matter how far away we sail, no matter how deep the waters, Vinnie is forever haunted.

In their eyes, my life growing up seems a fairytale and I, the prince. But it wasn't like that for me at all. My life has not been perfect, not by a long shot. This nightmare of a voyage is proof of that.

At eighteen I befriended, beguiled, and betrayed Catherine Garber, my soul mate. I deserted her, left her in tears, standing on the dock of the Cape Canal with my baby growing strong inside her. Catherine was convinced I was choosing a life at sea over life with her. Back then, I wouldn't (I couldn't) tell her the real reason I had to leave, but I have every intention of coming clean when I see her this time. How I'll explain Pitka—my marriage to her and our child—I haven't a clue. I had hoped the right words would come to me while on this voyage. So far, they haven't.

The truth is that I couldn't marry Cat and be a proper father to our baby because I had already committed myself to Pitka, a girl from the Yukon, whom I had also gotten in the family way and promised to marry. Pitka understood a sailor's way of life in ways someone as refined as Catherine never could have.

Leaving Cat was the hardest thing I've ever had to do, but it was the price I had to pay for my dual indiscretion. The burden on my conscience was lessened only in knowing that Will could provide Catherine with a better life. When I finally explain myself, Cat will tell me that this is a coward's reasoning. She believed then, and maybe still does, that our love would sustain us had my feet remained on solid ground. But I could not have stayed and been the same man, not even for her. Once she knows the whole truth, I'm sure she'll wonder why she ever loved me at all. But at least I'll get to meet my son.

Triton's Zodiac has seen better days. She's a 1925 Monterey clipper, a thirty-footer with a single-cylinder engine that runs on gasoline. Her owner was a landlubber and a drunkard. It was clear from the first time I laid eyes on her at the docks in Panama that she had been neglected. Besides being badly in need of a paint job, *Zodiac's* hull was encrusted with barnacles and creaked like an old man's joints. I was skeptical, but the owner was willing to drop the mooring lines in my hands in exchange for a few bucks to buy hooch. It would have proved a sweet deal had the weather cooperated.

The *Zodiac* has served us as well as a barroom wench—that is until the storm caught up to us and began beating down on her like a bat out of hell. We were urged to dock in ports along the route where we stopped for fuel and to sell off our catch, but this mission of mine is more of a driving force than the weather or the insurance of my own safety and that of my men. At the onset of the tempest, we were battling eight-to-ten-foot waves, soon increasing to twelve and fifteen footers that made us wish we had taken the advice of those who urged us to wait out the storm. By the time we sailed past Rhode Island our boat was challenged with waves so high, we were sure we were all but dead men. In all that time, not once did these mates so much as point a finger of blame in my direction. Thankfully, we're almost there; and I'm proud to be arriving on September twenty-first, just as my letter to Cat predicted I would.

A violent jolt rolls the boat, snapping me out of a pointless reverie. I brought along enough cash to treat the boys to three days of lobster fishing while I was getting acquainted with my unknown son, but now I wonder if we'll get our chance. For right now, it's all about survival.

We can barely breathe the air is so heavy with rain, salt foam, and fog. The sea and sky are one color, so that each time the *Zodiac* groans and rolls over on her side and the deck disappears beneath a cresting wave, we can't tell if we're up or down. Vinnie estimates the wind to be at 70 knots, strong enough to behead a fast-approaching comber and hurl its foaming tips at us at lightning speed. They shatter their liquid tonnage upon our desperate craft like massive sheets of glass.

The gods must be with us, for we have made it far enough to finally spot the unfailing rotation of the beacon light from Wings Lighthouse in the foggy distance. Like a helping hand it reaches out to guide us in, and I think for all our trying that *Zodiac* has pulled through for us.

But then, a rogue wave appears port side, daring us to climb its fatal wall. In the foggy illumination of the ship's searchlight, it looks to be roughly forty feet. I shout out a warning. Thomas comes up from down below, and Vinnie fights his way along the slippery deck to join us at the helm. Our string of curses can barely be heard above the deafening roar of the oncoming surge.

The *Zodiac* shimmies and shakes. I strain with the turning of the wheel, hoping to position her at an angle that might buffer the blow rather than risk a pitch-poll. We brace ourselves, hunching our shoulders so our necks won't snap like twigs and shut our eyes just as the *Zodiac* connects with the gargantuan wave. An icy mountain, as solid as a rock wall, hits our diminutive vessel, leaving us waist deep in water cold enough to paralyze. The windshield explodes, and razor-sharp shards of glass rain down on our heads, slicing our skin. It is a mortal wound for the *Zodiac*—a ship with no windshield is no match against a raging sea.

The boat rocks and lurches upward as the foaming flood above presses down upon the deck, rushing over and under the vessel's wooden railings. The electrical box that houses the transmitter wiring showers with sparks before finally sizzling out, leaving us in total darkness—and the gravest of danger.

Numb with cold, I find my footing and manage to secure the wheel with mooring rope to try and hold our position. I run the risk of the rudder losing control, but it's imperative we assess the damage.

Vinnie has already grabbed the emergency flashlights and together we jump below, holding our lights above Thomas, who disappears below water deep enough to cover his head and shoulders. He reappears in less than thirty seconds, spewing seawater and sputters:—

"Bit a hole in the hull! Bucket-bailing won't do it! She'll flood faster than we can empty her!"

The flooding of the ballast tank is instant suicide; I order Vinnie to grab a tarp.

"Aye, Cap," he croaks through lips already turning blue, and in two strides he is on the upper deck.

Thomas has freed the bait buckets. He shoves one in my hand and we bucket-bail together as fast as we can. More than working against time, we work against the probable hypothermia that will surely set in unless we can empty the water that is up to our knees.

Vinnie returns, dragging the heavy hemp canvas tarp. We stagger like drunks, each one praying to Christ that Thomas's transmission was picked up by the Coast Guard. If not, the three of us are as good as dead.

It takes the better part of two hours to stuff the hole with the tarp, and it's a patch job at best. The surge claimed our food and any supplies that weren't battened down. Soon it will drain us of body heat as well. Weak with hunger and badly fatigued, we huddle together like a wolf pack, keeping a constant lookout for a rescue boat. The leak in the hull has slowed some, but it will eventually take us down, and all three of us are experienced enough to know it.

While Thomas has the wheel, I slip my hand inside my rubber jacket and extract a tangle of red grosgrain ribbon from my shirt pocket. The frayed relic is wet, its ends flicking wildly in the wind. Crouching low, I hastily wrap it twice around my wrist with my free hand, tie it in a knot, and use my teeth to tighten it. I've kept the tattered trim for the past eighteen years—wherever I've sailed, wherever we've docked. If Catherine recognizes it from that long ago, I hope she sees it as an unspoken declaration of my love for her all these years.

I make my way along the slippery deck to replace Thomas at the wheel, shouting out for him to check our lifeline, and it's then that *Zodiac* suffers the second blow. This time the wave is bigger than the first by ten feet. I grab for the guardrail just as the bitch slams us broadside, snapping the *Zodiac* like a matchstick. I hold my breath in my lungs until I think they may explode; and when the wave finally passes over, I find myself hanging on to the bow for dear life. Flailing the water from my face, I frantically search around all sides, but the stern and my brave shipmates are nowhere to be seen.

Catherine

They arrived home yesterday looking like survivors of a war. William, Jonah, and Jack all safely delivered by the keeper of Wings Neck lighthouse. Bless Mr. Donnerman's soul for opening his door to four strangers and taking them in and giving them refuge. Later that night, he helped save Jack's life after Jonah and his father spotted him in the surf, wounded and clinging to a broken piece of hull.

Their lives were compromised during the rescue and precious time was lost while they waited out the storm and finally navigated their way to the home of a nearby physician, where the doctor determined Jack's internal injuries to be so severe he affirmed that there was nothing to be done to save him. I am told it was Jonah's near collapse that convinced William he should bring Jack to our home, where he would be cared for till the end and prayed for throughout that time.

It has been three days, and my heart is foolishly hopeful that Jack will pull through this. I place a bowl of soup on the nightstand and sit on the edge of Jonah's bed, where we have cleaned and tended to Jack's wounds and have laid him to rest comfortably. Ever so gently, I inch the bedding higher across the breadth of his chest, purposely brushing my fingers over the crop of soft, crisp hairs protruding from the open neckline of one of William's nightshirts. All too familiarly, I rest an open hand there that I might feel the beat of his heart pumping beneath it. I pray for every sporadic beat but discover each one to be more faint than the one before it; and in those fragmented seconds of an absent pulse, my eyes remain fixated on the ashen face of the man I never stopped loving.

I am quick to notice Jack's brow furrow slightly, and a weak cry escapes him as he struggles to awaken from the nightmare I imagine is haunting his dreams. My gentle coaxing eventually brings him around, though mirrored in his eyes, when he opens them, is a depth of pain I cannot bear to see him suffering. Yet, even in the throes of death, Jack's eyes are just as mysterious, just as dark, and just as compelling as I remember.

"Catherine," he whispers. It's all he can manage, but it is music to my ears. That he survived at all; that he is here with me now is almost enough.

"I'm right here," I say, rounding my hand on his cheek. His skin is cool to the touch, the stubble of his beard as harsh as sandpaper, but it feels like heaven to me.

As soon as they carried him through the door, nearly the first thing I noticed was that Jack was wearing a wedding band—a thin gold band that lost its luster long ago. Seeing it evoked such severe jealousy in me, I thought I would suffocate from the intensity of it. Now, after three days of staring at the wedding band on a dying man, I am resigned to the fact that Jack had married. Still, I'd sell my soul to know: *what it was about that girl that Jack would take a vow when he could not, he would not, pledge that same love to me?*

Tenderly, I dab Jack's lips with a soft napkin. Dehydration has left them cracked and peeling, and the napkin comes away bearing two tiny blood stains. I administer a dot of petroleum jelly, tracing his lips with my fingertip, grateful for this segment of time alone with him.

I brush aside a lock of shaggy hair from his furrowed brow and smile wanly. For now and until the angels carry his soul away, he is beautiful to me and in my safekeeping.

For days, William and Jonah have alternated being in the room with us and tending to Elizabeth, who has already witnessed enough devastation without having to witness a stranger dying. But when William enters the room this time and looks at Jack's fading pallor, he whispers that he is going to phone Benjamin Fromlehide and put him on notice—words I cannot bear to hear.

As soon as William leaves us, I take Jack's calloused right hand, with my red hair ribbon wound around the wrist, and lower my cheek to it. *He has worn this all these years,* I think, fresh tears springing to my eyes. Reverently, I lower my lips to the veined surface of the back of his hand, kissing it tenderly and breathing in the scent of his parched skin, so vaguely familiar.

The house is so still, so quiet, that the ticking of the hall clock reverberates. Its metronomic beat seems to be counting down the minutes of Jack's waning life; and I think to myself: *if only time could stand still. Better yet, if only it could be turned back!*

"Cat," Jack stirs. He tries to open his eyes. "So much to say...so sorry..."

"Hush now," I insist. "You must rest."

"Fine boy...," he breathes, "just...like Will."

"Handsome—like you," I say, tears running freely now.

In my grief, I am unaware that we are no longer alone until I feel my husband's hand upon my shoulder.

Jonah, too, has entered the room, with his sister in tow. I open my mouth to protest, but my son holds up his hand—a man's hand as of three days ago.

"She knows who he is, Mother, and she wants to be here," he says. Protectively, Jonah instructs Elizabeth to take William's hand and then he comes to stand at the bedside. He slides a small wooden crucifix from the pocket of his shirt and, touching it once to his lips, gently lifts Jack's fingers and tucks the cross beneath them.

We pray aloud as a family, but our prayers go unanswered. Within the hour, Jack's breathing becomes erratic. His eyelids flutter open; he looks first at Jonah, then at me. His eyes circle my face only once before his hand slips away from the crucifix; he is no longer looking at me but far beyond me.

Elizabeth bursts into tears, but William gently says to her:—

"Don't cry, Elizabeth. Jack is with his mates, now—they have come for him, you see, and are taking him home." Folding his hands in prayer, he continues:—

"Lord, with your grace Jack Wakefield and his friends will sail together once again, this time in the glorious Sea of Paradise, where no harm shall come to them, in the Glory of God, the Father."

Amen.

William

They say that a man is king of his castle. If that's true, why do I feel so powerless in mine? All I have ever asked of God was that Catherine should love me. I also prayed that He would call Jonah to take my place in a church I have taken and built up from the lost fold of congregants it used to be to the charitable, dedicated, and thriving parish it is today.

I have been a devoted husband and father. Jack's death has left me equally devastated, yet I have lent my support to Catherine with a genuine heart. I have carried more than my share of the load in order to give her time to come to terms with this tragic loss—and tragic is has been, especially with the chaos of having to locate Jack's employer to find out where to ship the body. Naturally, Catherine wanted him buried on Cape; but eventually she saw reason, agreeing that Jack's body belonged in Alaska, where his wife could grieve for him and give him a proper burial.

My prayer for Jonah to enter religious life never came to fruition, but I have made sure not to hold that against him. After all, serving one's country is more than a commendable profession. It calls for tremendous courage to be a soldier. I could never do what he will soon do, just as I could never help but love Jonah. He is easy to love, and I will go to my grave being a father to him, loving him as though he were my own. That's the way I have always thought of him.

Elizabeth, I'm afraid, is going to be the more challenging child. I remember Jack's father using a rather vulgar expression when we were growing up. Whenever Jack was trying to pull the wool over his father's eyes, the old man would say to him, "Don't piss on my leg and tell me it's raining!" Elizabeth *pisses* on my leg more often than not. Complicating matters is that she knows, just as her mother does, that the women in this household can wrap me around their little fingers. Her saving grace is that she is studious, never giving us anything serious to fret over. Academically she is at the top of her class and will hopefully have her choice in universities to attend. The world is our Lizzie's oyster. It always has been and probably always will be.

Catherine, who is both my rapture and my torture, fortunately possesses more of the former than the latter. Our marriage ebbs and flows, but only at best. If I had my druthers, both of us would have more passion—not only for life, but for each other. It is my constant prayer that one day this will be the case.

How many times in the course of our marriage have I had to have my own confession heard because I have wished Jack Wakefield dead? More often than I care to admit. Now that my wish has been granted, there are not enough confessionals, or clergy in them, to wash clean my tormented soul. There is only my own admission to myself which allows me to sleep at night: that Jack was everything and more than I credit him for having been. Catherine, however, will forever see him as someone akin to a god.

Certainly I, who had known Jack longer than anyone, other than his family, am aware of all he had going for him. Naturally, I do not admit this to Catherine. How can I tell her that I realize I am not enough for her—that I have always known that I fall short when compared to Jack Wakefield?

No one has ever thought to ask me why two lads as different as night and day became the best of buddies. I would have thought that Catherine would have been the one to inquire long ago, but she never has. I can draw from the archives of my mind, recalling the incident as if it happened only yesterday. We were but fourteen years old, Jack and I...

Lanky lads in knickers, dreaming big dreams—that's what we were, Jack and me. Where I was the voice of reason, always striving to do the right thing, Jack possessed the balls. Young as we were, he was the idol of every boy and girl in the neighborhood.

Despite Mr. Wakefield's prejudice, and naturally behind his father's back, Jack befriended a fourteen year old Negro boy named Amos

Browley. Amos was houseboy to the Romanos, a wealthy family from New Jersey that vacationed each summer on the Cape. The rumor around town was that Mr. Romano was 'connected.' Being a minister's son, I had no idea what that meant—Jack had to explain it to me. What we both knew for sure, however, was that Mr. Romano often took his belt (and fists) to Amos. The last time it happened Dr. Halston had to make a house call. Mr. Romano told the doctor that Amos had fallen from the limb of a tree in their yard; but Amos's older sister, Berta, told us the truth: Amos had been beaten so badly that when the doctor saw him, he had him rushed to the hospital, in Boston.

Amos had to be hospitalized for nearly two weeks. Jack was wild with rage. He demanded justice on Amos's behalf, saying Mr. Romano was going to pay for what he had done. When I asked Jack what he could possibly do about it, reminding him that if his own father found out he'd be in hot water, Jack told me not to worry; he'd take care of everything. Two days later, on a morning thick with fog, he made some lame excuse why he couldn't come out to play. I suspected he was up to no good, so I hid behind the bushes on the side of his house and, sure enough, Jack came outside not ten minutes later. He went into the shed behind his house and came out with his father's axe under one arm. Then he took off in the direction of the docks. I followed him there, taking care to keep my distance.

I watched as Jack first removed his shirt, then his belt, socks, and shoes. He unhitched his father's rowboat from its mooring and climbed into it, barefoot and bare-chested. I could see the young muscles across his back straining as he rowed; within minutes, the boat had disappeared into the fog.

Coming out from behind the shrubbery, I sat on the dock to wait. Eventually the fog lifted just enough that if I squinted, I could make out Jack's red rowboat stopping every few feet as it slowly made its way around the bow of the Romanos' seventy-two foot, triple-mast vessel, aptly named KING'S RANSOM, anchored there. Through the misty fog I could barely see Jack maneuvering the rowboat behind the craft where it disappeared for a long time. Had it not been for the distant chop-chopping echo of the axe biting into wood, I would have feared my friend and his boat were in danger. I remember my stomach kept growling from having missed breakfast, but I kept my mind off food by gathering stones and seeing how far I could skip them from where I stood.

187

Eventually, I spotted Jack coming out from behind the sail boat, rowing his way back to the dock. He saw me waiting for him but he didn't say a word about the deed. Instead, he tied the rope from his boat to the mooring. I stood above him on the dock, shaking my head with disapproval, my lips pressed tightly together. Jack said, "What are you, my conscience?" When I said I wasn't, he insisted I wipe the judgmental look off my face before he wiped it off for me.

Once Jack got over the fact that I had been spying on him, together we took immense pleasure in the sinking of Mr. Romano's boat. It began with a gentle rocking motion of the vessel from side to side until it eventually listed on its starboard side and stayed there, rapidly filling with water. We watched expectantly, two partners in crime, trusting the axe to have done its job. We didn't turn and walk away until seawater began filling the boat's portholes, ensuring us it would sink like a setting sun. Jack figured the bay would claim the luxury craft by nightfall; but by the look of things, we were fairly certain it wouldn't take that long.

We never thought that Jack's stunt would cost us our friendship with Amos; but Mr. Romano, furious that the Cape authorities could not find the vigilante responsible for sinking his prized possession, packed up his family and servants, bag and baggage, and hightailed it back to New Jersey.

"You can't ever tell anybody I did this," Jack had threatened that day.

"I won't," I promised, and I meant it.

"Swear," he ordered me.

"I swear it."

Jack reached into his wet trousers and brought out a small folding knife from his pocket. My empty stomach lurched, for I knew right away what he planned to do with it. Mustering up bravery I didn't feel, I extended my arm and squeezed my eyes tightly shut. Jack held my hand firmly in his, and I winced as I felt the sharp blade bite shallowly into the meaty flesh beneath my thumb. Nearly faint with fear, I somehow was able to perform the same ritual on Jack's hand. Then we gripped each other's thumbs, bonding the cuts together and making sure the droplets of blood from our wounds blended as one blood.

"Now we're blood brothers," Jack announced, looking into my eyes for confirmation. "You can never tell what happened here today."

"Yes, we're brothers," I echoed, "and I'll never tell a soul about today."

And I never did. All these years I've kept that story to myself. Recalling it now evokes a shame so deep that I hide my face in my hands and tremble with the memory of it. It is not being privy to the sinking of Romano's boat that has me guilt-ridden to this day, but for all the years that I have missed my best friend and never took the time to find him and tell him.

My feelings for Jack have run the gamut—from idol worship, to disgust, to hatred, and finally to feeling as though I am missing one of my limbs now that he is gone forever. So often I wished him dead. And now, he is.

My brother, my friend, forgive me.

Catherine

Three weeks ago today I would have said the sun would never shine again. But the tail of that horrific front delivered the most glorious weather, with a sky each day that looks as though Mother Nature has given it a rinse with a capful of Mrs. Stewart's Liquid Bluing. Majestic clouds now float in air made crisp and invigorating by the storm's passing through.

It is autumn at its best—just as long as you keep your eyes averted upward. To glance in any other direction would be to witness the demolition of a storm which, according to newspaper headlines and radio reporters claim, 'inflicted its wrathful fury along the entire eastern seaboard.'

On Long Island, where the hurricane first hit down, residents have dubbed it *The Long Island Express*. It began there and then continued a violent northeast journey through six more states before finally running out of steam somewhere over the Canadian border.

Since its occurrence, every local paper has been running cover stories about the more than seven hundred lives lost across seven states and the countless New England homes that were swept away or lifted and carried miles from their original locations.

Our own home has lost all its shutters; the railing on the widow's walk is gone, and shingles are missing from all four sides of the house. The porch is tilted, but at least the steps are intact. Trees are down, broken limbs scattered everywhere. What little lawn and garden we had is now ravaged. Of course, when measured against families who lost loved ones, property damages are less than inconsequential. Not only is it a tragic and depressing state of affairs, but everyone is frantic wondering where the funds will come from to pay for repairs.

The scents of mud and marsh, dead fish and rotting foliage assault us by day and by night. Area beaches, roadways, and miles of train tracks have been obliterated by the biggest storm of the twentieth century. Even some sturdily-built lighthouses and the dwellings, where the keepers resided, were wrecked and ruined. It was reported that even Rhode Island's Whale Rock lighthouse was literally swept off its base by the swells from the raging sea, claiming the life of the lighthouse keeper. It will be a year before all is righted. Only when I close my eyes and feel the cool autumn sea air blowing on my face and through my hair does it even remotely seem like the quaint, enchanting Cape Cod we all prided ourselves in boasting of.

Elizabeth is still having nightmares about that fateful night. I wake in the morning to find her curled like a cat on the hooked rug beside Jonah's now-empty bed. I wonder if her restless dreams are really all about the storm or whether they have more to do with her brother's absence.

William, who at first was right there for us, has become less able to offer us much support. His time has been divided between religious counseling for families who lost loved ones and volunteering with the Civilian Conservation Corps. He is but one of a throng of blessed men and women devoting what time and energy they can spare to the restoration of the eastern seaboard.

For my own part, I have organized a group of women volunteers to assist on the phone lines at the offices of New England Telephone Company. Operators are needed around the clock to man phones and to care for each other's children. Our efforts have been well received; though admittedly, I am keeping busy more for the sake of my own sanity than for the welfare of others.

Today it is my turn to watch the children whose mothers are working the phone lines. I have brought my charges to play in the nearby park, which looked far more inviting two weeks ago than it does now. Since the hurricane, any foliage that did manage to survive has turned brown. The park appears haunted and ghostly—washed out, except for the seesaw and two swings, which remained intact.

I observe the children as they play their innocent, childish games, envying their ability to laugh despite hard times. They run across a suffering landscape, oblivious to the fact that it has been reduced to half its size, and rally around a flag on a stick, which bears the emblem of the *Red Cross*. I am in mourning and feeling oddly detached from it all.

Edward obtained the services of Fromlehide Funeral Home to transport his aunt's body from Long Island back to here. How Frances would have gone on about it had she known she was the first to ride in the back of Benjamin's brand new hearse!

Naturally, William presided over her funeral service, most of which was an emotional blur for me. What I do recollect is how our little church was packed to bursting with mourners. Whether they knew her informally or for a long duration; whether their homes were in shambles or still standing, people came from far and wide to pay their respects to this great lady. It was Edward's intent that his aunt be laid to rest in Boston; but Frances, being obstinate as she was, made sure that her Will was uncompromised and was buried on Cape Cod.

Two days after the funeral for Frances, William again presided over a memorial service—this time for Jack, whose embalmed body was already on its way back to Alaska. In comparison to the turnout for Frances, Jack Wakefield's memorial service was poorly attended. He had been gone so long that he was barely remembered by the locals, and he had been predeceased by his parents. Although it was painful for the few of us there to see his memorial service so ill-attended, the service brought meaning to our grief, especially in the absence of a coffin.

September of '38 will go down in history as a month of loss for those states along the eastern seaboard. William and I were still reeling from attending funerals for several townspeople we knew who had died in the storm, only to have Jonah's enlistment day dawn swiftly. Even knowing all along the day was coming, there is nothing to prepare a mother for the moment her firstborn leaves home.

After losing both Jack and Frances, I would have sworn that there was nothing left of my heart to break. But the day Jonah boarded that train— William, Elizabeth and I watching him step up on the platform, looking every bit the patriot—what little heart I had left shattered, and there remains a deep void in my soul where my heart used to be.

In her absence, I have taken to spending a portion of free time each night sitting in Frances's living room, listening to records from her extensive collection and remembering our times spent memorizing every composition.

Tonight I'm so blue that I brought along a stale pack of cigarettes I found in Jonah's closet. Frances would have had a fit to see me smoking in her house, and my feeble attempt at it has me coughing. But the bitter taste seems to calm my nerves, and the filmy smoke adds a touch of melodrama in which to drape my lonliness.

If I've played it once, I have played it fifty times. Tommy Dorsey's sentimental ballad *Music, Maestro, Please* has my tears spilling over. When the song ends, and I lift the arm of the phonograph and lower the needle again at the start that I might hear the plaintive tune and doleful lyrics repeated.

> *Play your lilting melodies,*
> *Ragtime, Jazztime, Swing—*
> *Any old thing to help me ease the pain*
> *that solitude can bring...*

"Elizabeth is asking for you; she wants you to kiss her goodnight," William says, standing in the parlor doorway.

I had not heard his silent entrance, and I feel my shoulders droop with the burden of yet one more thing someone needs from me.

"Can't you do it?" I ask wearily.

"I *have* done it—every night for the past two weeks," he reminds me. "When do you intend to pull yourself together?"

"Soon," I lie, lighting a second cigarette with the stub of the first.

Agitated, William runs his hands through his hair and takes a seat opposite me. He opens his legs and rests his elbows on his knees. With his palms together and his fingers interlocked, he balances his chin on his knuckles and studies me as though I am an gospel reading he doesn't understand the meaning of.

"I am worried about you, Catherine, and I am not the only one who is."

"You have been discussing me?" I ask accusingly.

"No, but there are those who are concerned for you," he says.

"Like who?" I reach for the ashtray, but the long gray ash from my cigarette has already broken off and fallen on the rug. I brush it away with my foot.

"Benjamin, for one," he volunteers.

"I should think Benjamin Fromlehide would too busy counting the money he has made from this catastrophe to spend time talking about me—or anyone else for that matter."

William drops his hands in his lap. "That's a bit cold, Catherine, don't you think? Benjamin considers us dear friends and has suffered his own losses. You should appreciate his taking time to consider your welfare."

My look is somewhat contrite, but when I make no comment, William continues:—

"Perhaps you knew that Benjamin's sister runs a half-way house, in New Hampshire. We thought perhaps if you felt you needed a short rest—"

"I need *understanding*," I say, cutting him off. "Not only do I need understanding, but I could use some answers to some troubling questions—*that is all I need right now*."

"I'm trying to understand you," William says, "but you haven't exactly been making it easy for me. Tell me, what questions do you have? I'll try to answer them."

"I doubt you have the answers I'm looking for," I say, unwilling to cooperate.

William patiently waits for me to stop pouting and tell him what it is I want to know. The ticking of the mantel clock seems an amplified pounding in the stillness of the room. When he realizes I have no intention of elaborating, he stands up and comes to me with an outreach of his hand.

"Come," he says. "Elizabeth is waiting for us. Walk with me and I will tell you what you want to know."

I lift my face to him, wondering how he could possibly know what I'm thinking. He reaches down to assist me out of the chair as he notes my weariness. Together we leave the house, making sure the front door is locked behind us.

An evening breeze caresses us from behind as we turn onto the sidewalk and make our way back home. The street is still a sorry sight, although much of the debris has been removed. William must be able to hear my heart pounding in my chest; I can feel myself tight with pent-up resentment.

Apparently, my emotions are very transparent, for as promised, William says to me:—

"No, I do not know who Jack married, but I can tell you the reason he left..."

I am incredulous that my husband has read my mind. I stop walking and turn to him. "You mean, all this time you knew why and never told me?"

William looks unabashed. "It was between me and Jack—a conversation between best friends—and I gave him my word that I would never tell. As best friends, we had a right to our own relationship, separate and independent

195

of our friendship with you. I have thought all along that you were fairly content with me, Catherine, and the life we made together."

"I am, William, I swear I am!" I lean into him and lay my face against the warmth of his chest. He places his arm around my shoulders and rubs my arm.

"You are a better man than I deserve," I say, reveling in his support.

We stand this way for a few moments, supporting each other. I close my eyes and revel in the security of his protection. It is perhaps the first peaceful moment either of us has known in nearly a month's time, but then I move away and look at my husband with questioning eyes. William is trying to recollect the conversation so long ago between Jack and himself. Either that or he is thinking of how best to explain it. He says:—

"Before he left for Alaska, Jack confessed to being in love with you—" William reveals, "as if I didn't already know that! I remember looking at him in total disgust for what he had done to you. It made me sick to hear him out. In my mind, he was lowlier than low—a monster. And then he told me..." William struggles with the words, "he told me he had already put another girl in a family way."

I sway with the shock of his words, and William is quick to hold me steady. He guides me down our sidewalk and onto our porch, where we sit on the top step.

"Who was she? Who was the girl?" I ask, mortified.

"No one we know," William assures me. "I supposed her to be someone he met in port."

Before I can stop them, my tears have surfaced again, spilling down my cheeks, unchecked. I cannot afford to worry about William's opinion to my reaction, so devastated am I at hearing this news.

"Believe me, I was just as shocked to hear about it as you," he continues. "I had actually raised my fist and would have struck him, but Jack asked I hear him out. And so I did. He told me that he was only able to walk away from you because he knew I could provide for you a much better life than he ever could."

"Yes, he said as much to me on the day he left," I confirm. "But why did he choose *her?* What could she offer him that I could not?"

"The girl had nothing over you, Catherine, don't you understand? It was what *you* had over her—namely, a father who loved you, friends who cared about you, and *me.* You've always had me. The girl—whoever she was—had none of this. Jack told me as much."

"I-I don't know what to say—or if I even believe this," I admit.

"Well, it's true," William says. "Jack actually *entrusted* your wellbeing to me. He said that you and I represented everything good in this world and that we were worthy of a lifetime of happiness. I suppose that at that time, he knew he could never give you or Jonah the part of him he knew you both would eventually need."

"But he could give it to someone else—some girl he barely knew?"

"He wasn't destined to stay on the Cape, Catherine, even you know that. The girl—-some fisherman's daughter, he said—was already there. She was already living where he was going. I like to think that Jack believed his decision to be the right one at the time—not only for himself, but for everyone concerned."

It is as much as I imagine William knows or can explain in any further detail. He ends the conversation by telling me:—

"It's over, Catherine. Jack is gone."

And with those few words, I know it is true. A chapter has ended in the story of our lives, and I must finally agree to close the book.

William and I exchange a look as binding as any contract. My eyes tell him that any mention of Jack from now on will be for Jonah's benefit only. As we enter the house, I feel a pang of guilt to discover that Elizabeth has already gone to bed without a goodnight kiss from me.

We hang our coats and climb the stairs together. Lizzie is asleep, with the bedside lamp still lit. Her book, *The Secret of The Old Clock,* is tented open upon her chest. It is the first of the Nancy Drew Mystery Series, fifteen volumes of which Frances bequeathed to her.

Gently, William and I pull the covers up and over two tanned legs as spindly as those of a fawn. William shakes his head, bringing the fold of sheet upward to cover our daughter's arms. I smile to realize our Lizzie still enjoys getting giddy with her girlfriends. She still plays with her doll collection and loves to paint her toenails *Bubblegum Pink*. At least for now, with the worst behind us, our daughter has little to concern herself with other than the musings of fairytales and the frivolities of growing into womanhood.

I whisper to William that I wish to lie beside her for a bit, and he nods his understanding. He learned long ago from my relationship with Frances how females sometimes just need to share the space of another female.

I lower myself upon the bed and spoon against Elizabeth's sleeping form, feeling the locket Frances gave me shift beneath my blouse. William covers me gently with a light wool throw from the nearby chair. Bending first to kiss his daughter's cheek and then mine, William turns off the light and quietly slips from the room.

With the door partially closed, there is only a mellow wedge of light coming from the hall to share this united moment between mother and daughter. *Correction: Frances is here with us, too. I am sure of it.*

Jonah

At 0-600 the bugle will sound and me and my bunk buddies will hit the floor running. I've put in another restless night; I'll feel like a zombie when that horn goes off in two hours.

I'm lying on a stiff bunk, thinking about my life and the three-hundred and sixty-degree turn it has taken in the last month. In that short time, I have survived the storm of a lifetime, lost a father I never knew, got engaged to the best girl in the world, enlisted in the Navy, and inherited a house on Cape Cod. This last occurrence, having a small fortune attached to it, is thanks to a loving bequest from my so-called 'Aunt Frances,' who apparently felt obliged to reward me for saving her life when she suffered a stroke at home several years ago while I just happened by.

A week before I was to leave for the service, an official letter arrived from the law office of *Walker, Coffer & Reid,* requesting that my parents and I be present at the reading of a Last Will and Testament of Frances Wallingford Gellermont. I can still see Edward Wallingford's face, distorted with rage, as Philip Walker, Esquire read the Will. When it was over, Edward strutted over to me, putting his face within an inch of my own. With his lips tightly drawn, and drops of spittle landing on my shirt, he spoke just low enough so only I could hear:—

"I don't know what card you played in this game, McFarley, but I'll be damned if you'll take the prize. You're a sneaky little bastard. I'm going to contest my aunt's Will, and I'll win. And when I do, I'm going to take what's rightfully mine. You watch and see if I don't!"

His pretentious wife was standing off to the side, eavesdropping, while at the same time giving me the onceover. (I always thought Blanche Wallingford would give me a tumble if I had given her as much as an ounce of attention.) She had their screaming kid astride her hip. The child was whining incessantly, balling her tiny hands into fists, ready to flail out at anyone who tried to approach her. Collectively their anger was so apparent, it only served to convince me, and everyone else in the room that day, that Frances Wallingford Gellermont was of sound mind and body when she wrote her Last Will and Testament, and that she had intentionally 'put a fly in her family's soup tureen' by making sure the document was legally ironclad.

It will forever boggle my mind exactly why Aunt Frances thought enough of me and my fascination with the uncharted waters of forecasting to leave the bulk of her estate in my inexperienced hands. I have to believe she understood my passion; that all the time I spent discussing the dream Rachel and I have of one day devoting ourselves to this unexplored field of science had hit some chord of fascination with her. She understood my obsession to work with scientific minds—men such as storm tracker Charles Pierce, the young meteorologist whose on-the-mark prediction of the route of September's hurricane was overruled by senior members of the U.S Weather Bureau, and that many deaths could have been avoided had Pierce's bosses simply listened to the sound reasoning of a junior employee.

After The Great Hurricane, I wrote to Mr. Pierce to express my admiration and inform him of my intention to follow in his footsteps. I imagined the celebrated Mr. Pierce would simply see my fan letter as the insincere dream of a lad in search of a direction for his future. To my surprise, Charles Pierce sent a hand-written reply, encouraging me in every possible way to pursue my endeavor and asking that I keep him posted as to my progress. Imagine that!

While the inheritance from Aunt Frances is sweeter than sweet, it is at the same time humbling, especially since our country is on the brink of war. I am honest in saying that the money is secondary to the elation I have felt since Rachel accepted my proposal of marriage. Even though we all are still mourning the lost lives of those we knew and loved, our families cannot help but be happy for us.

Rachel thinks it especially romantic that I took her by surprise, stopping off in Rhode Island on my way to North Carolina. Stepping from the train that day, I witnessed damages there far more severe than what we had at home. Thankfully, the Coulters were one of the fortunate families whose houses were situated on an elevated lot and therefore did not fare as badly when the floods came. I was not surprised when a neighbor of theirs told me that the Coulters were downtown heading a crusade of relief volunteers. I went there and located Professor Coulter and asked for his daughter's hand before searching Rachel out and proposing to her on bended knee.

Hitler is on the march and a second world war is imminent, but Rachel and I plan to marry just as soon as she graduates from the university and I accumulate enough furlough to take her on a proper honeymoon. I admit it is a bit of a gloomy start, and certainly not how we dreamed it would be for us, but we are just naïve enough to believe we can sustain the hard times. Or maybe we are just young enough not to care.

Outside the barracks window a purple dawn is birthing, as pale as a bruise and as unobtrusive as a dream. The death mask of Jack Wakefield presents itself inside my head, where I imagine him fighting for his life—and those of his crewmen— upon a raging sea, whose death threat was impossible to gauge. I remember...

The Great Hurricane was barely finished ransacking the east coast and was slowly moving northward, where eventually it exhausted itself over Canada. My mother was half-mad with fear as she awaited some word from us, along with what news we had as to the whereabouts of a small fishing boat bound from Panama. Only with God's help were we delivered from the storm and later transported back home by the lighthouse keeper at Wings Neck, who had offered us refuge and ultimately saved our lives. It was my little sister, Lizzie, who recognized us when we returned home—-four men and a girl, climbing out of a stranger's truck, supporting between us the body of a legend.

In my opinion, Jack could not have asked for a nobler ending to his life. Even those of us who are soon to serve our country cannot trump a man willing to sail through hell, riding the back of the devil himself, in order to meet a child he's never known.

Since that fateful September day, both my parents have recited to me every story they can remember about their friend, and I find myself entangled in a web of imagination when I try to visualize this unsung hero and his deeds—both good and bad. The sharing of their stories have since empowered me, knowing I have Jack Wakefield's blood coursing through my veins, though I wonder if I will ever measure up to him.

The thought of another day of boot camp has my eyelids drooping with fatigue, but my mind can't help but think back to that time when I wished to be a fictional hero, such as *Horatio Hornblower* or *The Shadow.* Rather, I am privileged to be the son of a kind and caring preacher and the bravest woman I know. I am also the bloodline of the legendary Jack Wakefield: trickster, teacher, friend, and lover. My parents always said (as I later came to realize for myself) that Jack was an irresistibly fascinating man of dubious morality, whose greatest love, and most powerful foe, was the sea.

I flip onto my side and turn my back to the encroaching dawn. I use my shoulder to dig a comfortable niche in a mattress that is, by military standards, hard as a rock. I flatten my pillow and wedge it in the crook of my neck. I close my eyes. The air, filled with the musky aroma of male bodies confined in a barracks, is the smell that will be my companion for at least the next four years.

Eventually, the sandman pays me a house call, and I can feel a shroud of blissful sleep dragging me under. As I wearily succumb, my very last thought is that the bugle boy, who is probably stumbling out of bed right about now, will hopefully have great difficulty locating his blasted horn.

Epilogue
Boston, Massachusetts
May 1, 1945
Seven years after The Great Hurricane...

T he sight is perhaps the very juxtaposition of good and evil on Boston's Long Wharf ferry landing: A missionary nun in repose standing beside a newspaper boy selling *The Boston Daily Globe,* with its bold, shocking headline announcing Adolf Hitler's suicide.

"Adolf Hitler's dead! Read all about it!" bellows the scruffy lad, who is wearing a flat cap and flailing an issue of the day's paper high above his head.

With her own head bowed, the nun picks up her suitcase and steps away from the morose attraction to make her way down the dock. She spots a nearby bench, presently being occupied by a young woman whose nose is buried in a voluminous novel.

"Excuse me, might I join you?" the nun politely asks.

The occupant looks up. With her hand shielding her eyes, she sees the shrouded cleric radiantly outlined by the sun and immediately stands, nearly dropping her book. "Of course you may, Sister," she says, offering her seat and noting that the nun is but a few years her senior. "The ferry will be here shortly, but not soon enough that you would wish to stand to wait for it."

"Thank you," the nun says, wiping her perspired brow, "I am grateful for a reprieve." She lowers her suitcase to the ground, placing it safely beside the bench, and smoothing the back of her habit, seats herself at one end. She motions to the available space beside her with a dip of her veiled head, and then in traditional clerical fashion, tucks her hands inside her sleeves. The girl takes the proffered seat, once again situating the thick novel upon her lap.

"Pride and Prejudice is one of my favorites" the nun remarks, glancing at the title of the book, "and Elizabeth Bennet, every young girl's ideal."

"She is that," the girl beside her replies. "Miss Austen has portrayed a vivid character, though for all her intelligence and wit, Elizabeth Bennet has a tendency to judge immediately upon first impression; I try never to do that."

"Very wise," the nun agrees. "Do you live here in Boston?"

"No, Sister, I live on the Cape. Coincidentally, my name is Elizabeth, but my family calls me *Lizzie*."

"It's a pleasure to meet you. I am Sister Mary James, of the Maryknoll missionary."

Elizabeth inadvertently appraises the nun's modest habit, which has held a fascination for her since she sat down. She eyes the black veil with its stiff white edging and the long white tunic and waist-length cape, the fabric of which looks heavy to wear. She glances quickly at the Miraculous Medal hanging from a long chain around the nun's neck and notes the strand of rosary beads and crucifix that drape nearly to the hem of her robe, which Elizabeth wishes she could reach out and touch. "May I ask where your mission is located, Sister?" she asks instead.

"Ours was a small troupe of Brothers and Sisters based in Southern China," the nun replies. "We were there to preach the word of God and convert non-believers."

"Has the mission ended?"

"God's work never ends," the nun says. "Our mission worked among the poor and was making great strides until the outbreak of war, when we were threatened by a hostile takeover by Asian soldiers. Our choice was either to escape to the States or risk being captured and put to death. This has been a dark time for missionaries; but once peace has been restored, my fervent hope is to be reassigned."

"Then I hope this visit to the States will be a restful one for you," Elizabeth says kindly. "Cape Cod is like no other place, as you will soon see for yourself. Everyone there is very friendly."

"I have traveled a long way to get here," the nun tells her, "and so far, the journey has been pleasurable. Most people I've met along the way have been helpful, although most are reluctant to make conversation; it must be the habit."

She smiles and shrugs her shoulders, a sign of her own youth. "I'm glad that's not the case with us. Tell me, are you attending a university?"

"I'm a sophomore at Wellesley College, here in Massachusetts, working toward a degree in English literature, with a minor in journalism. After I graduate, I'll seek a position as a journalist. One day, if I write well enough, I hope to become a published author."

"Your parents must be very proud. To graduate from college with a double degree is no easy task," Sister Mary James remarks.

"They are proud enough, but I follow in the shadow of an older brother, who is extremely accomplished and already well situated. Thanks to him, there exists an elevated bar I must constantly strive to reach for."

"You look up to him, this brother of yours?"

"Oh, yes!" Elizabeth says. "At twenty five, he is a decorated war veteran and now holds an important position with the Weather Bureau, in Washington, thanks to a reference letter from Mr. Charles Pierce, himself!"

"So then, he was wounded in the war?" the nun asks, bowing her head and making the sign of the cross.

"He was, Sister—in 1941, aboard the U.S. destroyer, *Reuben James*. They were escorting a convoy to the United Kingdom when the ship was torpedoed in the waters near Iceland by a German U-552. Of the 159 men aboard, only 44 survived. My brother was among them, but he lost a leg due to complications from hypothermia."

"I am truly sorry," the nun says, "but how brave your brother was! We at home could never begin to repay those soldiers who have given so much to protect our freedom."

"That's very true," Elizabeth agrees. "Life improved for my brother, though. He married his childhood sweetheart; they have one son and another child on the way. He is also secure financially, thanks to the benevolent inheritance from a dear family friend, who helped fulfill his dream to become a weather forecaster." Elizabeth sighs. "Believe me when I say that I am in my brother's shadow."

"One could say that your brother has also been blessed," the nun suggests.

"Yes, but in fairness, no more than he deserves. He and our father had a terrible time of it in the hurricane of thirty-eight. They risked their lives trying to rescue a drowning man, and they were successful, but the man later died despite their efforts." Elizabeth, believing she sees the nun's face cloud over, changes the subject. "Oh, look," she says, pointing across the bay, "here comes the ferry!"

Both women stand to watch as the double-decker transporter makes its slow, deliberate trek toward the landing. In all the times Elizabeth has sailed on it, the sweeping line of the ferryboat never fails to impress her.

"Here, let me carry that for you, Sister," Elizabeth offers, freeing the nun of her luggage and bending slightly under its weight.

"If you wouldn't mind, might we sit on the top deck?" Sister Mary James asks. "I'd like to take advantage of the view on a day such as this."

They sandwich themselves between those passengers preferring the open air of the upper deck to the less-airy quarters below, making their stilted journey up the metal staircase. At the top, the two weave their way through the group until they emerge in the blinding sunlight of the upper deck.

Sister Mary James makes a visor with her hands over her eyes and looks upward to where the vessel's enormous double steam funnels and towering pole masts seemingly reach to heaven.

"I have always loved the ocean!" the nun exclaims, gripping the railing and filling her lungs with the scent of salty air. Her short veil streams out behind her, whipping in the wind. "If I had been born a boy, my parents would have let me choose my own path."

"What would you have done instead?" Elizabeth asks, clearly intrigued by the nun's confession.

"Oh, I had dreams of becoming a WAVE, but my father thought the military too dangerous a life for a girl. It would have pleased me to have served my country, especially during the war, as your brother did."

"Then it wasn't your choice to join the convent?" Elizabeth presses.

"Not at first; vocation was my parents' idea. My mother was a convert, whose religion was crucially important to her, and my father believed all clergy had been put on this earth to make up for sinners such as himself." The nun's features soften. "It wasn't until my first mission, when I began administering to the poor, that I truly understood why my father saw vocation as my destiny. Joining the missions would give to me the peace of mind he was never able to obtain for himself."

"I don't mean to pry, but was your father an unhappy man?" Elizabeth asks.

"He was more a tortured soul," the nun replies, "but he had his reasons."

Elizabeth is careful not to press further. "Surely he has peace of mind now that you willingly accepted the path he and your mother both wished for you."

"Unfortunately, my father died before I took my vows," Sister Mary James says matter-of-factly.

"Oh, dear," Elizabeth replies, wishing she had not brought up the subject at all. "Well, I'm sure he watched from heaven. I do know something about spirituality, after all—my father is a clergyman.

"A clergyman, you say? Would he happen to know a Reverend William McFarley, of the Bible Alliance Church?"

"Why, that's him! He is my father," Elizabeth exclaims, a look of total surprise lighting her face.

The nun is equally amazed. She asks, "And would your mother's name be Catherine?"

"It is," Elizabeth confirms, now even more perplexed, "but how would you know that?"

"Then the brother you spoke of is Jonah—Jonah McFarley," Sister Mary James concludes, completing her thought process.

Elizabeth shakes her head as if to clear it. "I can't believe this! How is it that you know my family?"

"To think that you and I have met here...like this..." Once again, Sister Mary James makes the sign of the cross. "Before God, this is nothing short of a miracle! My father often spoke of your parents when he told stories of his childhood." She takes the girl's hand. "Elizabeth, your father and brother...they saved my father's life! *He* was the drowning man they rescued seven years ago."

Elizabeth's mouth falls open as the pieces begin coming together. "That would make you Jonah's..."

"I am Jonah's half-sister; and by association, I suppose, yours as well. I was coming to Cape Cod in search of your family."

The nun looks up to heaven as if to give thanks to God then lowers her face until it is within inches of Elizabeth's own. She tells her:—

"My given name is Catherine," she says gently, casting an even smile at her new-found relative. "I am Catherine Wakefield!"